# THE PLACES WE SLEEP

# THE PLACES WE SLEEP

Caroline Brooks DuBois

 HOLIDAY HOUSE NEW YORK

Text copyright © 2020 by Caroline Brooks DuBois

Epigraph copyright © 2020 by Georgia O'Keefe Museum/Artists Rights Society (ARS), New York

All Rights Reserved

HOLIDAY HOUSE is registered in the U.S. Patent and Trademark Office.

Printed and bound in June 2020 at Maple Press, York, PA, USA.

www.holidayhouse.com

First Edition

1 3 5 7 9 10 8 6 4 2


Library of Congress Cataloging-in-Publication Data

Names: DuBois, Caroline Brooks, author.

Title: The places we sleep / by Caroline Brooks DuBois.

Description: First edition. | New York City : Holiday House, [2020] |
   Audience: Ages 8-12 | Audience: Grades 4-6 | Summary: Twelve-year-old
   Abbey's world is turned upside-down by both personal and national events
   of September 11, 2001, as well as their aftermath, but finds greater
   strength through art, friendship, and family.

Identifiers: LCCN 2019022768 | ISBN 9780823444212 (hardcover)

Subjects: LCSH: September 11 Terrorist Attacks, 2001—Juvenile fiction.
   CYAC: Novels in verse. | September 11 Terrorist Attacks, 2001—Fiction.
   Friendship—Fiction. | Families of military personnel—Fiction.
   Middle schools—Fiction. | Schools—Fiction. | Family
   life—Tennessee—Fiction. | Tennessee—Fiction.

Classification: LCC PZ7.5.D83 Pl 2020 | DDC [Fic]—dc23

LC record available at https://lccn.loc.gov/2019022768

For my parents, Jim and Rebecca Brooks,
and my 3 Rs, Richard, Rosabelle,
and Rowan, with love

Nobody sees a flower really; it is so small.
We haven't time, and to see takes time—
like to have a friend takes time.

~Georgia O'Keeffe

# SEPTEMBER

........................................................

1.

It arrives like a punch to the gut
        like a shove in the girls' room
                like a name I won't repeat.


It arrives like nobody's business, staring and glaring me down,
singling me out

             in the un-singular mob
that ebbs and flows and swells and grows
in the freshly painted, de-roached hallways of Henley Middle.

It arrives like a spotlight,
        like an intruder in my bedroom,
            like a meteor to my center of gravity.


It arrives.
And my body—
in cahoots—allows it.

                    Just.
                       Like.
                         That.

It arrives
and textbooks, full of themselves, weigh me down.
          This backpack holds the tools for my success,
yet I'm unprepared for IT:
No change of clothes,
no "girl supplies,"
no friend to ask
          because Camille is nowhere nearby,
no know-how,
no nothing.

*(Did I mention, it arrives like a double negative?)*

What was Mom thinking
by not thinking
to prepare me
for IT?


2.

The bully-of-a-bell taunts me,
rings its second warning
to those of us clogging the halls:

          *Follow the arrows, Dummy, on the walls!*
          *Remember your locker's secret code: 22 06 07*

Right,

Left,

and then Right again,

as if that cold metal box
holds all I need to survive
yet another school.

If I could just locate Camille—
        the only person I can talk to,
        the one friend I've made
        since we moved to town in June—
        *she* might know what to do.

But no sight of Camille's flame-red hair,
        and I'm pushed through the rush
of arms and legs and sideways scowls.
My insides turning black and blue;
my sense of direction confused,
just as the other new student—Jiman—breezes by,
head up and confident.
I stop to stare at her
        before stumbling in
to Ms. Dequire's room.
*Late again!* And her mouth forms its red-stained frown:

        "Tardy, Abbey!"

I find my seat, resist the urge to draw, instead
head my paper:

*Abbey Wood*
*Math*
*September 11, 2001*

3.

       I sit through that morning hour,
a dull ache in my abdomen
blossoming like a gigantic thorned flower,
jotting down mathematical formulas
I'm told are the key to my future.
Even with a math teacher for a mother,
my focus wavers in and out . . . until
       another teacher bursts in and whispers
       in the ear of our teacher,
       who stops teaching to wring her hands.

"Something's happening—in New York and in D.C.,"
       she informs us.

The tension is tangible.

"Some planes have crashed!"

But we don't know
       the half of it yet.

And to my shock,
we are soon released
                    from school.

Whatever's happening must be terrible.
But I can't curb my relief:

Early dismissal!
        Set free!

Free to trod off,
        free to go our separate ways

                like it was any
                            other
                                September day.

4.

        The buses pull up like salvation on wheels,
like rays of sunshine to my gloom.

        And Camille, my single friend in Tennessee,
is AWOL, so I sit up front on the bus and sketch.
Up front, with the kids from the elementary school next door.
Up front, with my back to kids my own age,
who are talking
and shouting

and pushing and shoving
and vibrating with questions about what's happening.
Up front,
where the driver is crying!

*Crying!*

> . . . *about what's happening in New York?*

> *New York is where Mom's sister,*
> *my Aunt Rose lives*
and Uncle Todd,
and my cousins Jackson and Kate!

If anyone has cause to cry, it's me—
> but I'm sure they're okay. New York is huge.

> It's not just that—my secret is now announcing itself,
and I have nothing to tie around my waist
> > and I'm wishing I hadn't worn white.

Maybe a few others have reasons too,
like the kid halfway back so short nobody sees him,
or the sixth-grader who sits near the football boys
and tries like mad to make them laugh.
Or Jiman, new like me,
> who also sits alone
> > but doesn't usually seem to care.

How will I walk away
from this bus, my back
to all these nosy faces,
eyes staring from windows,
arms dangling,
mouths jeering?

But I do.

And Mom's car is in the drive! The high school
must have been dismissed, too.

5.

It's the way she clutches the phone
and that unspeakable expression on her face—
her voice attempting to comfort
someone who is NOT me.
She glances, half-smiles out of habit
as I walk into our latest house.
But only her mouth smiles. Her eyes
are hollow wells of worry. Her eyes
miss the BIG change in me.
                    I need her
to hang up and follow me
to the bathroom,
to talk to me
through the door,

tell me, "Abbey, I'm here,"

but she doesn't.

I count to ten.
Breathe deeply.
Count again.

Is she talking to Aunt Rose? Uncle Todd?
Is it about New York?
      Her voice quivers and doesn't sound like her own.

      *What's going on there?*

**6.**

I soak my underclothes in soapy warmth
and think of the sink in my art teacher's class,
with its every-color splatter, and paint brushes
rinsing free of paint.

      The TV buzzes loud from our den
      with news of a magnitude I can't comprehend.

         Why can't Mom hear me
crying for her, needing her, screaming in my head—
the kind of screaming
a mother should hear?

## 1.

She finds me in bed,
sketchbook propped in my lap.

"Something's happened . . ." she whispers.

I rise and shadow her
     from room
          to room,
questions stick in my throat.

"My sister!" she chokes,
tossing random shirts
     and pants toward a suitcase
     and swiping at her eyes
     with a pair of socks.
I pick up clothes where they land,
fold them neatly,
place them gently
into her bag.

"What's going on—" I begin,

but she's distracted and tells me,

     "I have to request a sub,"
     replacing my words with hers.

I rearrange the photos of relatives on her dresser
and stare at a recent one
of my cousins.

Mom pauses packing for a few seconds,
looks directly at me and tries to explain
with plain language, straightforward,
seemingly simple:

*Your Aunt Rose is missing.*

Still, I stare,
my face a fill-in-the-blank,

my brain shuts down, my words dry up.

*Missing?*

*Missing* from her desk, her office in New York,
the towering building in which she worked,
but the building in which she worked,
her office, her desk are *also* missing,
as in—no longer.

*Missing?*

How can a building just give up,
be gone? How can people just disappear?

Mom is preparing
to drive to New York—
which is half a map from here—
to be with my cousins,
Jackson and Kate,
who are thirteen and eight,
and with my Uncle Todd,

while Dad and I
will be *missing*
her.

But not the same kind of *missing*.

My Aunt Rose is *missing* from the 86th floor
of a building that's smoldering and *missing*
most of itself.

      I visited her office once,
with my cousins and Uncle Todd.
See, my Aunt Rose and I,
we see eye to eye. We click.
She gets me. That day, she let me
sit in her chair and pretend to be Boss,
so I bossed everyone: *Be nice! Make art!*
Aunt Rose agreed, "Let's decree
*naps, music, candy—and raises
for everybody!*"

A framed landscape I'd drawn
decorated her office's white wall,
     which I guess
     is not there
     anymore.


8.

"All?" I ask.

"All planes are grounded," Mom repeats,
her voice gone monotone.

"As in, not in the air?" I ask again.

She nods, looks out our window
to the empty sky. "Who knows
what's coming next!"

After planning her route, she hesitates—"Your dad
will be home soon"—and then kisses me,
grabs her final necessities,
and loads her car.

I remind her to wear her seatbelt,
to call when she gets there,
then I wave goodbye,

but she's already in math-teacher
problem-solving mode.

      In comparison, my problem shrinks
to beyond microscopic, so I befriend
the bathroom.

Beneath the sink, Mom's supplies
loom like a commercial
for a product I can't decode.

The folded, illustrated instructions,
black-and-white line drawings
of a woman who smiles with knowledge
she won't share
      with a girl like me.

The woman, all curves and experience,
could help me if she wanted,
but she doesn't. And nothing Mom owns
works for me.

These bathroom walls offer no advice,
the green carpet as useless
as grass in a house.

The bulbs around the mirror glare,
illuminating my ignorance.

I'm the star of this one-character show,

but my freckles look like dirt
and the trash can fills up
like failure

—and Mom is driving out of town this very minute.
She is going,

going,

gone.

## 9.

I call Camille,
visualize her phone
echoing in her empty home.
If she's shooting hoops, she won't hear.
If she's not home, she won't know
that I've called, since I leave no message.
I'm just a phone ringing,
echoing in somebody's home.
Unanswered.
Unheard.
Alone.

## 10.

Later that evening,
from my savings
I pocket seven bucks

and catch a ride with Dad, who's camouflaged in fatigues.
Since Mom's left town,
he's on a mission to buy us food
so he won't have to feed me MREs—
the military's version
of instant meals.

On the drive, he doesn't speculate
on what President Bush should do—
or mention anything about anything really.
I guess we're both in shock.
His silence fills the car. He steers
us toward the store, as if that's all
he remembers how to do.

      The rest plays out like a nightmare,
      a slow-motion blur of shame,
      that begins with me slinking the aisles
      of mysterious hygiene products,
      skipping over a box like Mom's,
      hoping not to see anyone I recognize,
      looking no one in the eyes,
      and avoiding Dad, who's lost in his head
      and wandering frozen foods.
      Then I snatch a box of pads from a shelf
      and dump too much money at the first register I find
      and turn and run
      with the guy calling after:

"Hey there!
You! GIRL!"

Dad,
with his special-op skills
and his empty hands
and an unreadable expression on his face,
regards me with my purchase
so visible,
so obvious.
So!

And his voice turns to whisper
as he finds his words
and shakes his head:
"Today is like nothing
I've ever seen."
              I freeze at first,
              but of course I know
he's talking about New York,
Pennsylvania,
and D.C.

Not
me.

## 11.

Our father-daughter time we spend
glued to the *tube*, as Dad likes to call
our TV—

the FIRST plane
　　　　soaring, angling, drifting
　　　　　　　　　　　　　birdlike
　　　　in the blue-sky, sunny,
ordinary morning.

The plane is low, banking,
　　　　　　turning,
　　　　　　　　　then plunging
　　　　　　its knife
into the north tower.

Debris and papers
　　　　　　fluttering free,
　　　　　　　　among the shock and disbelief,
　　　　　SHOUTS,
　　　confusion, panic.

That's when a SECOND plane
　　　　　　　　careens
　　　　　　　　　　　　into the south tower.

                              Cursive
                      plumes
                of
            smoke
drawing
an
upward
line.

People exiting,
                fleeing,
                        men and women
                              workers and visitors running,
stumbling, dazed,
afraid.

Then,
        a THIRD plane slams the Pentagon—
fueling angry flames.

C
  o
  l
  l
  a
  p
  s
  e
of the first tower.

A FOURTH plane smacks
                    ground in another state.


The
coll-
            apse
                    of the second tower.


These
things
we
can't
un-
see.



12.


Morning arrives
regardless
and finds me Momless.
*Planes fell from the sky!*
*You'd think they'd close the schools.*
But not here.

Dad says they're aiming for "normal"—
                    as if middle school is ever that.

I bet there's no school for days
>in New York.


So like any other Wednesday, it's
sun up,
>get up,
>>get ready.
One foot in front of the other.
"You know the drill!" Dad barks.


>*But has anyone found Aunt Rose?*
>Images from the TV footage replay in my head.


I yank the spotted sheets from my bed
and feed them to the washing machine.


Twice, I scour my hands,
but the feelings don't wash away.


Usually Dad
>is THE ONE out of town,
>on a mission—a top-secret this or that.


But here we are together—him, me, and the silence
at the kitchen table.
Just the three of us!
>I picture Mom driving north, biting her nails into oblivion.
Dad sounds nervous when he speaks in my direction:

"Do you . . . *need* anything?"
He must've seen through my grocery store charade
and called Mom last night.

*Yes!* I want to shout
with two competing thoughts: *I need you. I don't need you.*

Then I second-guess myself:
*Does he mean breakfast?*

"I'm good. I've got . . . what I need," I mutter,
trying to disappear,
and hoping he's not talking about
what I think
he's talking about.

Seconds later, he jumps when the phone rings,
acts surprised that it's Mom, hands me the phone
too delicately, as if avoiding contact.

Mom's distracted—so many miles away—
but tries to sound positive.

I can tell by her voice that she knows:
"Abbey, sweetheart . . . welcome!
It's your entry
into womanhood!"

But as I sit there clutching the phone,
lonely
is all I feel.


13.

As if it couldn't get worse,
Dad returns from his bedroom
holding a book—A BOOK!—
with a faded, outdated cover.

"Your mom told me you should—uh—
read this, I guess," he grunts
in his serious Sergeant's voice.
Then he stands there staring into his coffee.
And I stare at the book
as my face
ignites.

*Are You There God? It's Me, Margaret.*
Margaret looks more secure
                              than I've ever felt.


        "It was your mom's," he offers,
planting his palm gently on top of my head,
as if he could press down
and hold me at this height
forever.

14.

In my backpack,
I conceal the girl stuff
like foreigners among the pencils,
gum wrappers, and notebooks.
Like flags of surrender
like wings separated from the butterfly,
like little white handkerchiefs,
like folded notes
never to be postmarked.
　　　The word SANITARY
imprinted loudly in my head,
making my skin crawl.
　　　What's sanitary
about this silent
siege
on my body?


15.

In Ms. Dequire's room, some boys
actually sound elated: "Did you see them fall?"
"KABOOM!" they say, making planes
with their hands.

I avoid eye contact, look away, escape
into my head. But at a school this small,
you can't escape being new.

I scan the halls for the other new girl, Jiman,
and am struck by her solemn appearance,
eyes cast low and serious.

      Does she know someone in New York, too?

         I wonder to myself
       *What did Aunt Rose do?*

*Was she aware,*

        *unaware,*

            *have time to prepare?*
*Type an e-mail,*

     *make a call,*

         *run or scream or cry,*
    *take the elevator,*

           *take the stairs,*

*have time to think, to blink,*

*time to wish, to wonder,*

*did someone help her,*

        *was she alone,*
     *did she whisper a prayer,*

*close her eyes,*
*glimpse the pictures*
*on her desk*
*and on her wall?*

*And where*
        *is she now?*


16.

Like a shadow on an overcast day,
        staring at my own two feet,
        I walk at a distance behind Camille,
        steal peeks at her and her teammates,
                her friends from before we met.


She doesn't know I'm back here
        and there're twenty-some people between us—
        or she'd wave me into her crowd
and link her arm through mine.


She's just one of those people—
everybody likes her,
except maybe The Trio,
who just like each other.


Jiman walks by herself like me,
the smile she's worn since August is gone,
her eyes dart side to side
                as she takes
                        careful
                                nervous
                                        steps.

While battling my locker,
I overhear Camille's other friend,
her neighbor Jacob,
say, "Where's *Whatserface*,
                    that new girl who's always drawing?"

And Camille,
in her singsong voice, reply:
"Her name's Abbey. Learn it. Use it!"
            Then teasingly,
"She could teach *you*
a thing or two
about art!"

I smile despite myself.
I've never made such a good friend
so quickly.


17.

Even with Camille,
I can't shake what I feel:
I'm still *that girl*—
the one who doesn't belong,
not fully alone,
but surrounded enough to have to try
to fit in, to blend,
like oil paint
and water.

Art
has always been my thing
from school to school,
but maybe here in Tennessee,
maybe now,
it's not enough.
I want to be known.
I want to be
seen.

I'm used to
the adjusting,
starting over, the beginning
again, others passing by me
staring through me,
or asking
   *Who're you?*

I worry about people speaking to me
and worry just the same
when they don't.

Sometimes, I think
I might blow away
like autumn leaves,
like ashes from a fire,
like sheets of paper
from a spiral
as I trip and stumble,

try to hold it together
like some pre-teen
Humpty Dumpty
just beginning
to crack.


18.

I lug my backpack
to every subject,
the zipper's smile—
tight and toothy—
protecting my backup
stash. I minimize
my movements, aim for
inconspicuous, stay
in my lane, hope no
one notices how
every hour or two
I leave class.

Then
Ms. Dequire
actually complains
to the whole class,
"*Again*, Abbey?"
and sighs
dramatically.

## 19.

Some kids at Henley
resemble kids from my previous schools,
from each state
where Dad has been stationed.

I used to rattle off
all of my schools
like a chant I'd memorized for class
or a mnemonic device
like "The Presidents Song."
        But the schools are beginning to blur,
and I think I've forgotten a few.

It's hard to keep my own history straight
now that the school count
totals over eight.

        From first grade until now,
I've known six Blakes—
five that were boys
and one Blake girl.

        I hear that name *now* in the hall,
and turn, expecting one of the Blakes
from before.
But it's a new Blake,
a new face
to learn.

Maybe there's another Abbey here already
at Henley.

At my last school,
most of the parents
were also Army,
just like Dad.
But Henley's far from the base.

Mom planned it that way this time,
to live like the longtime residents
in a civilian neighborhood,
without the coming and going
of people and their stuff
that occurs when you live
on a base.

It might've been easier
to be just *one*
of many Army Abbeys
in a school
filled with other
Army kids.

## 20.

It took me exactly one week, four days precisely,
to meet *The Trio* of Henley Middle:

Sheila, Angela, Lana

Angela, Lana, Sheila

Lana, Sheila, Angela

The first few weeks, I confused their names.
But now, like everyone else,
I know their flawless faces
and can place their voices
from around any corner.

When they saunter down the hall,
hip-to-hip-to-hip,
you have to scoot way over
to let them pass.
They *won't* see you.

If one wears teal, the others do too.
If one skips lunch, the others do too.
If the football boys sneeze, The Trio coos, "Bless you!"
If one scoffs at you,
the whole school
scoffs too.

21.

On the bus, I update Camille.
      tell her about Aunt Rose—
      at least all I currently know—
      which is
           nothing.

      We scrunch down low in the seat,
knees against the bench in front of us
as if holding it up.

"That's terrible!" she exclaims.
"My parents are donating their blood."

      "And there's something else," I whisper,
      "I
           got
               IT!"

Then my only friend in Tennessee
studies me as if I'm somebody
she's just met.

      "IT?" she whispers back.

"IT!" I confirm.

And after a pause, she beams:
"I could tell you were different!"

"That obvious?" I groan.

"It's just that I *know* you!" She grins.

I stare at her briefly,
not sure how I got so lucky.

"Pretty sure The Trio have it, too," she adds.

"Great!" I roll my eyes.
"I'm in a club!"

We erupt in laughter—
the kind that turns to tears—
as others on the bus
stare at where we sit,
but I don't care
because we're just two voices floating up and out
the half-lowered,
rectangular
windows.

## 22.

Down the aisle of the bus, I wobble
with a smidgeon more confidence than before,
and just as I turn to wave at Camille,
who makes a *Call me*
gesture with her hand,

"Army brat!" is spat
from the mouth of somebody I pass.
        That's how we described ourselves
at some of my other schools—but *this* doesn't feel
like *that* now, this label that's not my name.
I spot Jacob, Camille's neighbor,
and a pack of smirking boys at the back
who start to snicker.

To my surprise, Jiman
suddenly seems to see me,
looks directly in my eyes and semi-smiles

        just as I bolt past her.

Or did I imagine that?

Maybe she was smiling
                    to herself.

The confusion I feel
is for real
and can't be erased
from my easy-to-read
open-book
face.

23.

At home, I perch on the corner of the couch,
behind my hair and my latest sketch.
I draw when I can't handle my thoughts, imagine my art
hanging somewhere cool, like the school's hallway,
with a circle of friends surrounding me,
saying, "Nice work, Abbey!"

Dad sits like the Lincoln Memorial,
upright in his reclining chair.

He's purchased some "female gear"
and deposited it, in a brown paper bag,
on my bed while I was at school.
Beside it, he's placed a new sketchbook.

Neither of us mentions this.
Instead, we choose to stare straight ahead.

Still no sight of Aunt Rose's face on the TV.

The 24-hour coverage shocks and shocks:
the Twin Towers collapsing into themselves,
the dark cloud hovering, people fleeing,
and the planes crashing over and over again,
as if perhaps *this time* by accident
but aimed so perfectly.

"I just don't get it," I whisper.

"They're terrorists," Dad tells me,
matter-of-factly, but his voice catches
and he coughs
and switches the channel again.

New York has never seemed so close—
yet Mom so far.

On another station, they say:
"We've been attacked on our own soil."

      I know a few things about war,
from Dad—
Germany, Hiroshima, Vietnam,
but not *here*.

      "You shouldn't be watching this." Dad finally snaps
it off, grabs his combat boots to polish
since it's something he can do with his hands.

I know he wishes he were there,
in New York. Instead of here,
with me.


24.

On the phone,
Camille makes small talk and tries to cheer me up:

"You move a lot! That's all *Army brat* means.
It was probably one of those jocks at the back.
Or one of The Trio—Angela was back there.
She's probably just jealous."

"Yeah, right!" I sigh
and kick a pillow from my bed, thinking of Mom
and Aunt Rose and Uncle Todd and my cousins
in New York, and trying to recall
if the voice on the bus belonged to a girl or a boy.
I don't mention that Jacob was among them
since I know how Camille feels about him.

"How do people know my dad's Army?"

"Henley's small, Abbey,
and lots of people around here are Army.
Plus, it's obvious—
you're a world traveler.
You've been places.
Look at me! I've never
left this Podunkville."

"Yeah, but at this rate, *I'll* have whiplash
by high school."

25.

*My dictionary offers up all it knows:*

1. brat /brat/ - noun. somebody, especially a child, who is regarded as tiresomely demanding and selfish in a childish way

2. brat /brat/ - noun. the son or daughter of a serving member of one of the armed forces

*which is really nothing,*
*more or less what I already knew.*

26.

In a dream,
I'm falling,
like a body from a building,
falling away from something I need to hold on to,
falling from an unfathomable height,
falling away from others,
from the faces I recognize—
pushed to the edge of bleachers,
out of group pictures,
squeezed to the back of lines,
staring from a car's rear window
as we drive away again
from everything
I think
I know.

## 27.

We fold name tents today.
Some teachers still don't know our names.
One called me Amber twice the other day,
and the gym teacher just calls me "You!"

> *Crease the paper hot-dog style.*
> *Write your name big and bold.*
> *Place it at the front of your desk.*
> *Use it in each class.*

I write ABBEY—colorful and cheerful.
But it might as well say *New Girl*
because that's what half
the class calls me.

I notice Jiman's composure
when she's called upon, how she shakes her hair
from her shoulders, lifts her head up
like she doesn't mind being new and unknown.
And when a teacher mispronounces her name,
Jiman simply corrects her, without apology,
but respectfully, politely—and even
the teacher seems impressed.

## 28.

Our teachers try to discuss
what's happened—the attack

on our nation.

In Art, Mr. Lydon asks us to *paint* our emotions.

I choose red and black
to smear across my bone-white paper
because that's how I feel.

He pauses behind my easel and studies my work,
my hands become birds and I start to tremble.
But when he moves on, I feel invisible.

Camille paints the shape of the Pentagon with colors that run
off the page.

Tommy watches Sheila paint New York's *new* skyline.

Assuming the role of *Most Talented*,
Jiman paints the coolest flag I've ever seen,
with abstract stars and stripes outside the rectangle.

But then in the lunch line,
one kid says to another, right in front of her,

"They should all go back to where they came from!"

And I see Jiman freeze,
a carton of milk squeezed
in her hand
    and I think I hear her whisper
        *I am Muslim*
            *but also American.*


    Later in Social Studies, we read stories
about the man who crossed a tightrope between the Twin Towers,
      the man who parachuted from the north tower,
         and the man who scaled the south one.


Mrs. Baker asks,
"Who here has visited New York?"


My head pounds
    as I try *not* to think of Mom
    so far away.


Then Camille, with her talky-talk mouth,
can't help but proudly inform the class:
"Abbey's mom is there right now."


Someone coughs, "Big deal!"


*Thanks, Camille!*
for building my fan club
one card-carrying member at a time.

"Do tell, Abbey!" Mrs. Baker prompts me,
after glancing again
at my name tent.

Through clenched teeth
I inform the class,
            "My aunt is missing—"
        and everyone turns and stares
and demands to know more.
Suddenly I can't swallow, can't breathe,
feel my heart speed up
a few beats.

*I have a captive audience!*
*And I've forgotten how to speak.*
*And the sound of my own voice*
*out loud in the classroom*
*is terrifying.*

## 29.

I have to ask for the hall pass *again*.
Each and every bathroom knows me now.
This is the one where *Sheila Loves Tommy!*
is scrawled on a stall door.
        Before, I'd never considered the disposal
boxes, their creaky lids, the loud crumpling
that paper makes, the dispenser by the sink

hanging loose from the wall, the mirrors
reflecting, or mocking me—hung too high
to help, if I need to check my clothes.


30.

In Music, we sing "America the Beautiful."
I feel dizzy and mumble the words
and find myself wondering
what "God shed His grace on thee" really means.

Across from me, Camille sings her heart out,
eyes closed, face beaming, mouth wide—
fearless personified.

*That is so like Aunt Rose!*

A tear runs down my cheek,
                    and I shove it aside.

        Aunt Rose lives and breathes music.
It's not what she does for money
but what she does for love. She once
told me, "Abbey, I'd rather sing than talk."
Plus, she hums nonstop—
            and plays more instruments than I can count: piano, guitar,
            violin, harmonica, and even drums.

Mom always says, "Rose is the creative one,
and I'm the mathematical one."

*I want to be just like Aunt Rose.*

Once in their New York apartment, I broke a maraca
while marching in a pretend parade
with my cousins Jackson and Kate.
The tiny pellets scattered
from one end of their apartment to the other—
rolling away lickety-split.

I can still hear Aunt Rose proclaiming:

> "Let the music spread.
> Little seeds for new melodies!"

A sob now catches in my throat.

*That's just how she is!*

*Or should I say—was?*

My mind
is
stuck
in
present
tense.

## 31.

The past seems so far from today.
But only one month ago,
we were at the beach.
And my cousins and I
built a towering castle of sand
as tall as Kate.
Until the tide came
and stole it away.

## 32.

On the school bus
after school,
I spy Jiman
who appears comfortable
sitting alone.
I sketch her,
wish I could be
more like her.

*Jiman,*
an illustration of confidence.

I repeat her name in my head.

*Jiman,*
a portrait study in nonchalance.

She's new to Tennessee. Just like me.
She sits alone. I sit alone, too,
but a microphone and spotlight
seem to amplify and highlight
*my* every unsure
move.

I wonder if Jiman
notices me, wonder if she observes
the war the football boys wage
on the weak.

I glance quickly
in their direction.
They are all eyes
and busy mouths
when they spot me
and bust out laughing
and whisper things,
then laugh some more.

I let my hair fall
curtain-like across my face.
*Show's over!* I think
and push forward and off
that rotten,
stinking
bus.

## 33.

I used to think "stationed"
meant staying put,
like the word "stationary,"
but I was wrong.
It's more like a brief rest,
then a forwarding address,
and time to learn a new zip code
—and way of life—
all over again.

If it weren't for Camille,
I'd be ready to pack up,
disappear. Be gone.
But this time, when my family moves,
I have so much to lose.

      Our current house is painted
a greenish-brown, and it's at least
twenty miles from the base,
which is now on
*High Alert!*

"Security's tight!" Dad explains.

He's awaiting his orders.

      I can't recall all of my previous bedrooms.
This one here is pink.

So random it seems, the places we sleep.
I place a thick towel between me
and my clean sheets.

I've been staring at this ceiling
since the beginning of summer,
since back in June,
when Dad got stationed in Tennessee.

Mom and I are stationed here, too.

The last state was South Carolina,
and before that
it was
Colorado.

34.

Today Ms. Dequire
sends me to the school nurse,
convinced I have a bladder infection,
and I can't find the words
to disagree.

Her closet of a room is papered
with rainbows and food charts,
and she explains, "Abbey, I'm here to help."

So slowly I begin,

"I got my—" thankfully she knows where I'm going with this
and pulls out a picture of the pelvic region
from a drawer in her desk.
She names a few body parts.

And I cringe at each.

Then she points to the two
fallopian tubes, and my mind drifts
to the Twin Towers and New York,
where Mom now sleeps.


Finally she asks, "Do you have any questions for me?"
I pause . . .

then begin, "I *have* been wondering
when it *all* will end . . ."

And for a second or two,
the nurse just stares, as if I'm asking
about something else entirely, as if I've asked
something too personal, a question for which
there's no answer. Her hesitation
makes me fidget with the hall pass.

"My mom . . . just left . . . and I—
I'm just ready for it to end."
I drop my shoulders
and begin to cry in this tiny room
with this total stranger.


*Then, guess what?*
The nurse, smelling of powder and bread, hugs me,

and it feels good,
and I hug her back—
      and I believe she needed it, too.

And we sit there hugging like idiots
for a full minute or two.
      Then she hands me a tissue and says,
"It's monthly, about four to seven days each cycle.
That's not too bad, is it?"


## 35.

In the bus lines after school, when Angela and Lana
point to me and announce,


      "New girl's got a DISEASE that Nurse can't cure!"


to everyone who's around to hear,
including Jacob and the back-of-the-bus boys,
Camille marches up
      in their puffed-up, lip-glossed faces
      and says exactly what she thinks:


      "If anyone's got a disease, it's *you*!
      A disease of the heart.
      Doctors say yours are missing."


      And that's why
Camille is my all-time best friend—

even over Makayla in South Carolina,
and Lisa in Colorado.
I'd even go so far as saying
we're like blood sisters,
but without the blood,
unless you count the colors of red
flushed through our faces right now—
hers shining like courage,
and mine a mixture
of embarrassment
and pride.


## 36.

On the bus,
Camille beams,
pumped up by her victory:
        "Did you see their smiles vanish?"

"You have a way with words," I agree.

"I do, it's true." She closes her eyes,
lays her head on my shoulder—
affection comes so easy
for her.

I take in the moment, soak it up.
This is what having a true best friend feels like.

"Why doesn't Jacob
ride the bus much?" eventually I ask,
remembering her other best friend
and all the boys
who witnessed the scene
just now.

"He does. Sometimes." Camille yawns
catlike in the afternoon sun.

Camille and Jacob have been friends
since forever, even though he's a year older.
They play basketball or soccer in her backyard
most afternoons—and have done so for years.
And although I haven't known Camille
for near that long, and I don't play sports,
I knew the minute we met at the community pool
this summer that we'd be good friends too.

She bounced right up to me at the snack bar,
dripping water and out of breath,
and exclaimed, "I love your swimsuit!
I'm Camille. Who're you?"

That's all it took!

*We just knew.*

I pause my thoughts

when we come to my stop,
say goodbye to Camille
and jump up to leave.

But once again,
I'm caught off guard
as I file forward
to exit the bus

and a boy's foot juts out

and trips me up.

*On purpose?*

*Maybe*
*it's*
*new kid*
*target*
*practice.*

It happens so quickly,
I barely catch myself.

As I collect my stuff,
he mumbles to himself, "Didn't even
see you there!"
like I don't
exist.

## 37.

Dad tapes the MISSING flyer
Mom sent of Aunt Rose
to the refrigerator,
beside a permission slip,
shopping lists,
and photos.

*Are you really missing*
*if you don't wander off in the woods,*
*get snatched in the mall, or run away?*

I can't help but think of stranger danger
and *America's Most Wanted.*

Uncle Todd took that picture.
Aunt Rose is smiling at him, in their kitchen.
Jackson and Kate make faces behind her.
I can almost hear her voice—she was saying:
"Hurry up! Take the picture!
My cookies are burning."

Then afterward, she dashed to rescue
the sugar cookies from the oven.
A treat because *I* was visiting!

She didn't know then
that now she'd be missing.

I study her face, fear her features
will fade until the picture
is all that's left
of that memory.

On news shows,
fences are papered with flyers like Aunt Rose's,
like yard-sale signs or concert posters.
The flyers multiply like a quilt of worry
sewn by loved ones: pictures from weddings,
graduations, birthdays, ordinary days—
faces smiling,
smiling,
smiling.

All those happy faces.

38.

On a certain show,
I hear a phrase
for the very first time:
                    "Human remains."

        And it sounds like humans
who stay behind—a hopeful sign of people alive.

Then the true meaning sinks in—

*They may not find Aunt Rose.*

Without warning,
there's pressure in my chest
like I might explode.

I call the New York apartment,
hoping to hear Mom's voice,
but Jackson answers instead.

"She's out for groceries, I think.
      You want to speak to my dad . . . or Kate
or—" then his voice dies out,
and I realize he was going to say "my mom,"
so quickly I tell him,
"I'd love to speak to Kate."

"Sure."

And then . . .

after a lengthy pause,

"Hi, Abbey," says a tiny voice on the other end.

We speak for a bit
but after a while,
I can't think of anything
much to say,

Then, I'm all smiles.
A huge, dumb grin in fact—
so relieved it won't be me or Mom,

happy not to be leaving Camille . . . not yet at least.

    "I just want to prepare you," he says,
    trying again, seeming confused
    by my happiness.

Then he just sits there
turning that poodle around
in his big,
strong
hands.

40.

"Artists have a story to tell,"
Mr. Lydon informs the class.
"They keep telling it
until they get it right.
They must take risks.
Trust themselves!"

Jiman, across the room,
listens intently to Mr. Lydon
and dares to paint over her first attempt,

and the silence
slinks in.

"Tell my mom I called, okay?"

And the words "my mom"
feel terribly wrong,
like I've said or done
something hurtful.

39.

Dad sits down at the bottom of my bed.
It sags with his weight.
He wants to talk.

*Please don't be about my period.*
*Or the pads he bought.*
    *Anything but that!*

    "There's a chance . . ." he begins,
    ". . . that I may get mobilized." He holds
    Mr. Poodle, my purple stuffed dog, in his hands
    and turns him around and around.

"If you mean move again,
I won't!"

"Nope. Just *me* this time around."

trusting herself, her instincts. New paints,
clean brush—and she's in her element.
I watch,
how one painting hides another
layered just beneath it
and even another
beneath that. The way a face
can hide a person's entire life,
a story no one knows, a history untold,
until someone seeks
to share it.

I get up and cross behind Jiman, drawn
to her painting. She pauses brush midair.
Heads turn, ears tune in
and a hush falls over the room—

                                   but I scurry on,
the moment gone, the status quo resumed,
my courage dried up like ancient paint.

## 41.

For P.E.,
we all stumble and push into the locker room
to claim any private spot to change
into our gym clothes. The walls seem to sweat
with our arrival. Some girls seize

the mirrors, brushing and pulling
at their hair. Angela and Sheila assume
center stage and strip off their shirts and pants,
not bothering to cover or hide themselves.
Sheila's bra is lavender, Angela's is pink.
Sheila has breasts already and flaunts them.

> "Ohmygod, I'm a cow," some girl whines.
> "Moo!" another laughs.

Some of us wait in line for a stall, like Camille,
who stopped changing in front of others
on the day Lana remarked:
> "I don't know why *you* need a bra."

Everyone is edgy and impatient;
you'd think we were waiting to be fed
the way we eye one another. But we wait
like *good girls*, not cutting in line.

Lana stands too close behind me,
rolling her eyes and trying to grab
Sheila and Angela's attention.

When a door swings open
and Jiman steps out,
Lana shoves me toward her,
says, "Geez! Go in already!"
then wrinkles her nose at Jiman,

who looks the other way
and doesn't let Lana
get to her.

I lock the door and yank off my jeans—
exposed,
in my plain underwear.

I follow my new feminine ritual
of protecting my gym clothes from myself,
but take too long,
                    my movements jumpy and jittery.

Through the door, a slice of yellow
is all I can spy of Lana's shirt.
Then her shoe begins to tap,

                    tap,

                              tap

and her voice begins scoffing, megaphone-loud,
"Hurry up! WHAT
are you *doing*
in there?"

42.

Later that week,
Ms. Johnson gives us each a yellow ribbon
since we're studying symbolism,
and we're sent outside to find a suitable tree

somewhere on the school's property
around which to tie our hope.

I notice Jiman is absent,
hear rumors that someone spray-painted words
on her parents' restaurant,
and I wonder what they wrote
and why they would do it.

Sheila and Angela tie their ribbons
around the same tree,
and when Sheila commands:
"Tomorrow, Ange,
let's wear red, white, and blue,"
Angela responds, "Sure, Shee-Shee."

For a second, I wonder
if I should wear those colors too.
Then I look for Camille, who waves at me
as she heads off on her own,
her ribbon fluttering
wild and free.

Beside the ball field,
I find a solitary tree with drooping leaves
and lots of low branches.
Last summer, I would've called it
the perfect climbing tree

—but I'm no longer Abbey

who climbs trees.
The Trio would say,
*That's for babies!*
I extend
my arms around its width,
and the bark is rough and scratches me
as I tie a lopsided bow
and whisper,

"This is for you, Aunt Rose."


## 43.

My period ends—finally!
                  Over. Period.
                            The end!
                    In the first grade,
              Mrs. Bennet taught me:
"End a sentence with a full stop
so the next one can begin."
And after seven long days
that felt like years,
I am me again
I guess, but
I feel like
one huge
question

mark.

44.

After a few days,
Jiman is back at school.
On the bus,
she settles
directly
in front of me.
I say her name
in my head
the way I've heard
her say it.
It's lovely
and suits
her.

Up close,
she looks smaller.
I stare at the back
of her head. Her hair
waves in mahogany layers
and smells of lemons.
She holds her chin high again
and doesn't hide.
        *I* am the new kid who
cowers, emotes, reacts—
and the boys at the back
can sense that.

Camille
is a "car rider" today,
so I'm extra afraid
to shift or make a sound.
I try NOT
to breathe
too loudly.

Jiman sketches
and seems content,
even dares
to open a window
and let the wind
rearrange her hair.

I smile despite myself,
imagining us as friends—
*Jiman, Camille, and me!*

That's when the boys sit up,
take notice of my goofy grin.
Too late to hide it behind my hand
as they start to chant
    Ar-my!
      Ar-my!
        Ar-my!
BRAT! BRAT! BRAT!

Then it hits me
like a putdown on a playground:
I've been invisible
at more than one school
but never a target like this.
To all, my biography reads
as whatserface, newcomer, girl
from somewhere else
other than here.

I stand to flee
and see a picture
Jiman was drawing
unfinished in her hand
of a little leafless tree.
She turns to look at me
with maybe care
or concern
on her face.

Tears cloud my vision
and my feet do a tango
with my backpack
and everyone observes it all
with their bulging eyes,
as I stumble up the aisle,
trying like mad
to escape
my never-ending

social
demise.


45.

*Mom*
remains in New York.
A sub teaches her math classes
at the high school.
Jackson and Kate must need her.
Uncle Todd must too.
I don't know what's happened to Aunt Rose.
At night, Dad and I stare at the TV,
eating macaroni and cheese.
A woman reports, "New York is crying,"
and I look at Dad for his take on this.
He keeps watching.
I imagine big tears spilling
from skyscraper windows—
falling and splashing
and washing away
the soot and ash
and cleansing
the streets and people
and Jackson and Kate
and Uncle Todd
and Mom
until everything sparkles—

bright and shiny,
like
new.


## 46.

A few days later,
Mom comes home to us.
She squeezes me until I can't breathe
and drops her bags and collapses
      into Dad's arms,
           and then onto our couch.

I sit on the floor at her side.
"How're Jackson and Kate?"

She brushes the hair from my face.

"Todd can't stop looking,"
she says, mostly to Dad,
who stands and paces,
and leans hard against the wall.

To me, she whispers,
      "I love you,"
and kisses my hair.

Gently, she turns my face to hers.

My tears are stuck
somewhere deep inside.
      Perhaps I'm Abbey
who no longer cries.

Then, as if waking
from a dream, she asks,
      "How have *you* been?"

The football boys on the bus
spring to mind
and their unwanted attention,
and how my period arrived,
and how I just want to find
a place to belong.

I glance at Dad
still holding the house up
and answer
with the first words that come:
"I've survived," I say, sounding
like a more mature Abbey,
even to me.

Then—
      an aching
          moment
             of SILENCE

f
  a
    l
      l
        s

          over us
          like a heavy blanket of rubble
and my cheeks burn with what I've said
and I cannot breathe
with the weight of my stupidity.

    *Aunt Rose*

Dad looks from me to Mom
        and then back to me, then tries
to change the subject.

"It's okay," Mom whispers,
patting the couch
for me to sit
beside her.

"I'm sorry I wasn't here."

I rest slightly against her,
closing my eyes.

      If I don't open them
ever again, I could be *that girl*—

the one in our home videos,
the one with pigtails,
who skins her knee and cries to be held,
who doesn't know about terrorists,
whose aunt is still alive,
who holds her mom's hand.
That version.
That girl.
That one.


## 47.

Murmurs escape
their bedroom—
details they won't share
about Aunt Rose. I know
from the sound of their movements
Mom is unpacking, pulling
clothes from her bags,
dumping them onto the bed.
She seems to have misplaced something
          or left something in New York.
The few words I catch
are like pieces of a puzzle,
a code to crack: ". . . right here . . ."
Panic rising in her voice,
          ". . . must have lost it!"
          Then Dad's voice trying to calm her,
and then hers again: "God! Where is it?"

Now she's crying, now weeping,
and louder still. She's gasping
and saying, ". . . the letter . . . the last thing she wrote . . .
Todd gave it—to me."

I freeze, motionless in the hall, listening . . .
as if my stillness
will help her find
whatever she's missing.

And in that stillness,
I imagine my uncle,
the firemen and rescue workers,
even Jackson and Kate
searching through metal and concrete,
their hands scraped and dirty,
bloody, searching for something,
anything to grab onto,
to pull up and out
of the darkness
and into the light
of breathable
air.

48.

I yank my thoughts back from New York.
Here in Tennessee, I could be "Abbi" or maybe "Abs."
A talented artist, like Jiman. I could be an athlete

like Camille or Jacob—no trash that!
Just somebody people know.
I'm so over just being *new*!

From here forward,
one thing's for certain,
I'll be *Abbey*
*who gets her period.*

 And maybe I'm imagining things,
but Sheila, Angela, and Lana
have begun to regard me a little differently,
like there's a neon sign on my head
that everyone can read: *Look at me!*
And I know Camille didn't tell.
Maybe my trip to the nurse
tipped everyone off.
 In the halls,
some boys glance at me, glance at my body

. . . or perhaps
 it's all in my head.
and no one
is thinking
anything
about me

at all.

## 49.

At least
I've found a friend like Camille.

*Camille,*

who loves basketball
whose limbs are lean and athletic
whose red hair waves out of control
who sings without fear
who talks without self-censorship
who doesn't seem to care
what she wears
or who likes her
or how she moves between groups
or through the halls
or what anyone thinks,

*My* friend.

## 50.

In the cafeteria, locker room, halls,
on the school grounds outside,
everywhere kids are discussing
what will happen next—
which U.S. cities are potential targets,
if the president makes an easy mark,

if they will bomb Oak Ridge,
which is not too far from here.

Maybe it's all in my mind,
but I think this school's coming together a bit
in the wake of such a tragic event.
Some cliques are un-cliquing.
Maybe I'm even starting to fit.
I saw a member of the Geek Club—
kids who play chess and take Advanced Math—
talking with a cheerleader yesterday in homeroom
and planning a community vigil.
Even Camille's neighbor Jacob
seems to see me
as we pass between classes.
He once even asked about my aunt.

      And today at lunch,
the-one-and-only Sheila
sits beside ME, actually confides in *me*,
while opening a lime yogurt,

      "My mom and dad and I are *never* going overseas again."
She scans the room for her counterparts,
then continues, "Our travel agent
is changing our summer destination
to Charleston, where we can at least
trust the waiters and chefs
not to poison us!"

      Then for some reason,
      she stops talking

long enough to glare
over where Jiman sits.

"Cool!" I say, trying to relate to her plans.
Though I've lived many places,
I've never thought of them
as *destinations*.

Red, white, and blue banners
have taken over the school's walls.
One reads "We Love America!"
It's like how everyone felt
when Henley's basketball team
scrimmaged Hargood Middle—
united.

Us against *Them*.

But who are *they* anyway?
Even Mrs. Baker, our social studies teacher,
can't explain.

When the other two-thirds of The Trio appear,
Sheila excuses herself,
doesn't acknowledge me
as I wave goodbye
to their retreating
backsides.

51.

Football Tommy boasts
to anyone who will listen
how his father is buying a gun
and a gas mask and building
a bunker beneath their house
where they can live for 45 days
on cans of green beans
and powdered milk
and bottled water.

Camille's dad
labels himself a *pacifist*,
condemns both the terrorist attacks
AND
the imminent war.

My dad watches TV,
observes an anti-war march
in downtown Washington, D.C.—
just 18 days after 9/11.
"They're against military action,"
he says. And then, "It's not my job
to agree or disagree. Someone
has to protect
our country."

# OCTOBER

......................................................

52.

As *if* life is back on track,
as if buildings haven't fallen, and people haven't disappeared,
as if the world isn't torn in two about going to war,
Camille and I crash at her house
to get down to solving homework equations.
We settle ourselves in her bedroom,
where sports stars beam from posters,
and pictures she colored when she was five
surround her mirror, and a growth chart
climbs up her wall to her current height.
I pull a neglected My Pretty Pony
from under her bed and braid its hair.

> Camille has lived her *entire* life right in this spot—
> and Jacob has *always* lived next door.

Her bedroom is *so* Camille.


We finish our math and head outside
to shoot hoops in her backyard.


After a few misses, I locate chalk
in her garage and sketch our names—
> cursive and temporary—
onto her driveway:


*Abbey*     +     *Camille*

She holds the ball
to watch me draw our faces.

"I swear, you'll be famous one day!"

"You can come
to all my art openings
in New York and in Paris."

"Gladly!
And you can come
to *all* my games.
          She dribbles!
          She aims!
          She shoots!" Camille announces
as the ball swishes
through
the
net.

"Any word on your aunt yet?" she asks casually—
or cautiously—
and a little out of breath.

All I can do is shake my head.

"I'm sorry,"
she says between dribbles.

And I know she means it.

53.

Someone whistles
from a window next door.

It's Jacob.

He leans out,
waves his hand,
and calls Camille's
name.

A minute later,
he's standing beside us,
a soccer ball tucked under one arm
and a basketball under the other.

He studies my drawings
and raises his eyebrows.
       But I don't know how to interpret this.
       He looks at me not too differently
       from the boys in the halls.
But the boys who taunt me
hijack my mind
and how he's probably overheard
what they've said.

It's hard to know how he feels,
read what he thinks,
since sometimes he hangs with the other athletes.
Maybe he agrees, believes
I'm a brat too,
just like they say.

Then my tongue
goes all chalky
and suddenly no one is talking
and I have nothing to do with my hands,
so I smudge the faces I've drawn
with the tip of my shoe
and whisper,
"Gotta run!" and dash,
like I tend to do lately,
leaving them
staring
after
me.

## 54.

On October 7th,
close to 12,000 people
in New York City

m     a     r     C     H

from Union Square
                    to Times Square
in opposition
to the administration's
War on
Terrorism.

Camille says
her dad wishes
he could join them.
She tells me that instead
he marched around
their block.


## 55.

At home,
some days Mom buries herself
in stacks of math tests at the table,
red slashes here and there
on her hands from grading.
I feel sorry for her students.

I walk through rooms
and she doesn't look up.
Once, she turned off the light
as she left a room
that I was in.

Other days, she slouches
on the couch, a glass of red wine
in one hand, a photo album open
on her lap, Aunt Rose smiling from photos.
I close the book when she drifts off,
pour the wine down the sink,
and lay a blanket
over her.

When he's home,
Dad lingers
at the doorways of rooms
and occasionally asks her,
    "Is there anything you need me to do?"
or he studies news programs,
as if hearing people talk about "suicide missions"
will tell him
how to fix this—

and Mom.

## 56.

We attend the vigil
held at the fire department.
A patriotic song is sung.
Flags of all sizes are flown.
The adults are crying,
except Mom, who is too sad

to be here. Strangers hold
hands, hold on to each other,
hold each other's babies.
Dad and I don't know how
to be sad together,
so we smile and pretend
to watch children
turn cartwheels in the grass.
I'm sure he's wishing
I was still one of them.


57.

I'm attempting to sketch the still life
Mr. Lydon has arranged
in the center of our classroom.

He's explaining how you have secondary colors
*because of* the primary ones.

Jiman's sketch
looks just like a photograph.
I wonder how
she did it.

I find nothing inspiring
about the bowl of fruit
but try to capture the shades of apple
versus banana.

I bet the *fruit* find themselves boring too!

When Mr. Lydon isn't looking,
Tommy snags an apple
and chomps it.

> *How are we supposed*
> *to keep this up*
> *with the world*
> *crumbling*
> *around us?*

I imagine the fruit bowl imploding, apples
spinning away, bananas
smashed—
            and find myself needing to know
if everything has a purpose,
a place and a plan
on this planet . . .

Suddenly
Mr. Lydon approaches,
making his rounds behind us.

I hunker down . . .
            then he's directly behind me
and I blurt out:
            "What's a . . . *suicide mission*?"

Other kids are shocked
at my voice—
          probably me more than them.

Without pause—and as if it's on topic—
he says, "An act that usually takes the life
of the perpetrator as well as others,"
and then he changes the subject:
          "I believe you've found
your medium, Abbey. Colored pencils
are working out well for you."

"Thanks," I mumble
and turn back
to the apples and bananas,
          wondering what cause
could be worth
all those lives.
And what caused me
to let the random thoughts
out of my head.

Camille looks over
and mouths, "Your medium!"
And my cheeks turn
the Magic Magenta
pencil #7 color.

## 58.

In the hallway
between Science
and Language Arts,
Jiman appears
and pauses directly
in front of me, eyebrows
raised in recognition.
I come to a sudden stop.
Mirror-like, we move
in whatever direction
the other one starts—
her eyes laugh at this.
But it's no surprise that
I'm overcome by self-doubt
and flee before I find
any words
to speak.


## 59.

I dream
Dad and I
are shopping for groceries.

In the produce section,
I spy Mr. Lydon,
so naturally I cower

behind the broccoli, blushing
from head to toe.

He holds up a kiwi and muses
to no one in particular:
"You'd never know it's green in there!"

Dad quirks his face
at a man pondering the color of fruit,
then fires commands at me:
"Abbey, front and center!
ASAP. Pronto!"

I creep forward,
and we push our cart
loaded with duct tape and plastic wrap
away from Mr. Lydon.

      The dream then shifts
like a TV channel changing
from a cooking show to a broadcast of war,
in which Dad takes cover from gunfire
like an actor in a desert scene
        but it is too real
        and I wake drenched
in sweat
and
fear.

60.

Today we're driving to New York
for Aunt Rose's *memorial.*

       Any other time, I'd be thrilled to miss school.
You don't have to be good at math to know

          new school + new girl = new ways daily to be mortified.

Mom likes *her* school and hopes I like Henley too,
since she was unhappy in our previous states:
"Tennessee will be good for the Woods!"
But the best thing here so far is Camille.

We're headed out of this state now
               to where sadness awaits.

I've never seen a dead body before,
except on TV.
And never anyone I loved.

       Mom informs me there will be *no* body

and that her parents, Grandma Jill and Grandpa Paul,
will be there.

Dad drives while Mom mostly sleeps.
He curses the other cars

that drive too slow or too fast
or generally do something wrong.

He points out the sights and landmarks:
"The majestic Smoky Mountains!"

"Look—a herd of deer!"

"Check out the Potomac River."

I watch it all slide by
and sketch the passing hills,
a barn, other people in cars,
a church.

Stopped in traffic,
Dad peers over his shoulder at me
and calls me "Abbey the Artist,"
so I tilt the sketchpad up for him to see.
"It's my medium," I tell him shyly,
displaying a green pencil.

"Is that right?" he asks before turning back
to the road, to the world of signs
and speed limits
and solid lines
adults aren't supposed
to cross.

## 61.

A car is a good vehicle
             for daydreaming
with stock scenery rolling by.


I summon Jacob and Camille,
imagine them playing basketball,
passing and shooting and doing
all the things best friends do—
like they did before I arrived,
like they'll do again when I move—
             then *I* am there with them
and Jacob tosses me the ball.
To ME of all people!
Just like I'm one of them,
but my hands are full of art supplies
and I drop it all—even daydreams should be semi-realistic—
and Jacob stops playing
to go all day-dreamy:
             "Can I help you with that, Abbey?"


But before I know it,
we're in New York already,
and Mom is getting out of the car
without looking back.


And it's hard to hit *Replay*
on a daydream.

62.

We eat Chinese,
the three of us, like old times, but quieter,
a restaurant we'd eaten at once for Christmas
       with Aunt Rose and Uncle Todd.

       Jackson, Kate, and I had drawn on the placemats
and folded them into airplanes
       and sent them innocently sailing
          across the empty restaurant.

The place hasn't changed a bit,
but the world has.

63.

The next day,
I stand apart from my cousins
who stare at their feet and cry,
surrounded by whispering,
sniffling, Kleenex-clutching adults
and emotional hugging
and "I'm so sorry"
and ridiculous bouquets
of beautiful flowers.

Jackson wears a tie,
which strikes me
as funny
            and I want to pull it,
but I know
            he won't chase after me today.

Kate, only eight, seems older than the last time I saw her—
almost older than I am now.
She stands amazingly still for her age—
no wiggling or twisting, no falling down,
no yanking at her clothes.

It's confusing to see them
without Aunt Rose,
who was always there—
dancing with us, handing us
bags of popcorn, singing silly songs,
or putting a Band-Aid
on someone's knee.

I don't know what to say,
so I say "Wow!"
and point to all the flowers,
but Jackson and Kate
just stare harder at their feet,
and wipe their faces with their hands,
as they stand side by side
like sad dolls in fancy clothes.

The words

*Red Rover, Red Rover, send Abbey right over*

pop into my head, but I cannot
join my cousins
or snap them out of their grief.

They're brother and sister—

and *I* am just a girl
whose mother is somewhere
nearby.

64.

Back at their apartment,
casseroles and tiny sandwiches
crowd every empty surface.

Who *are* all these people
who knew Aunt Rose?
Did they work with her in the tower?
If so, how did *they* escape?
A sobbing woman
corners and tries to hug me,
but I slip away.

I've always thought of the instruments
throughout their apartment
as my aunt's friends.
I don't even know what she did
at her job. It must have been important,
enough to die.

Uncle Todd just stares,
standing stationary in their living room,
the center of a shifting group.

He's skinnier than I remember
and his beard is growing in.

He doesn't call me "Abbey Fabulous!"
like he used to, but smiles vaguely,
as if thinking, "Who are *you* again?"

Jackson seems to shrink back
from him, as if it would hurt
too much to touch.
If ever there was a time
they need Aunt Rose,
it is now.

She was their cheerleader,
their tour guide, the captain
of their joyride—and now they are adrift.

She was the mom who lived for
roller coasters, screaming louder
than all the others, painted her toenails
a rainbow of colors, made
a family of themed costumes
for Halloween.

      Grandma Jill and Grandpa Paul slump
on the couch, silent tears
trail down their faces.
I sit on the couch's arm.
Grandma smiles up at me
and grabs my hand.

We watch all the people.
Some are eating.
Some talk quietly.
Dad, for once, seems to know
*just* what to do and stands close
to Uncle Todd, as if to catch him
if he falls. Mom scoops up Kate
and places her on her lap
with a book in front of them,
      and I'm glad she does this.

Someone plays Aunt Rose's piano.
I keep thinking it is her
and looking over my shoulder.

> Was Aunt Rose the last person
to touch the keys? It angers me
that it can make music still.

## 65.

It's different this time
with Jackson and Kate.
> Usually, we fall instantly in sync,
tumble off to build a pillow-and-blanket fort,
or write a play, or plot a rolled-sock war,
or color tattoos on our arms
for our rock-and-roll band:

> *Introducing The Donuts!*

"You can tell *they're* related,"
> our parents would muse from another room.

We just fit together—like Legos.

We were "The Three Musketeers!"

This time, though, they seem
more like names or familiar faces—
two people I see a few times each year,
to whom I happen
to be related.

After a while, they retreat
to their bedrooms
and close their doors.

Is this what *heartbroken* looks like?

      On a napkin, I sketch a heart
fracturing and falling apart
into two piles of red.

On the long ride home,
we pass the same landmarks—
the same hills,

            towns,

                cities,

                    bridges,

                      and rivers.

I stare out the windows.
Again, Mom sleeps while Dad drives
and curses the other drivers,
      yet somehow this time
I find a little comfort
in all this.

## 66.

My period comes 'round again
like a nightmare

like a surprise test in Science
like a speech I have to give on a stage
like a recurring dream
with people I cannot locate
and something important I've forgotten to do
and blood on my hands that will not wash away
and a familiar stab
in my lower back.

I hug myself into morning,
doing the math:

7 days
Once a month
12 times a year

7 x 12 = 84 days a year

*I want to stay in bed,*
*stay home from school,*
*skip my entire seventh-grade year—*
but I hear Mom leaving
for the high school, her car backing
down and out the drive, and this
feels like my cue
to rise.

Sometimes, lately, she forgets
to wake or kiss me before she goes.

It's okay, though;
I'm a young woman now.
I should be able to deal with this.
It's only middle-school
after all.


**67.**

"A portrait should capture the heart of a person."
—Mr. Lydon

In Art, I draw my first
                    self-portrait:

Roundish face. No, stretch that longer—
oval, pale-moon face.

Long sweeping hair,
tree-bark brown—no, coffee brown—no, grizzly bear brown,
the kind of brown that sweeps across your face
and tries to hide what you're feeling.

> Dark eyes like secrets,
> like lockets that hold
> how you feel about yourself
> and all the places you've lived,
> the friends you've left—
> Makayla was the hardest to leave.

She made you laugh out loud when no one else could.
She was silly, and silly was good.
But Lisa was a good listener
and made the best s'mores
and cried when you moved.

An ordinary, nothing-special, speckled nose.

A mouth that wants to say something to someone—
but mostly stays quiet and closed.

Signed

*Whatserface*

68.

"Nice picture . . . Abbey!"

    Jacob calls
        from somewhere behind me
                in the hall.

I freeze
    and turn—

and almost drop the portrait.

*He knows my name!*

"You know my name," I manage,

       hiding my mouth behind my portrait.

"Of course! You're Camille's
*other* best friend."
He grins.


## 69.

Dad's on the base all the time now,
so when I need anything, I have to ask Mom.
She's agreed to take Camille and me shopping for shoes,
but I'm afraid she's forgotten
or gone all zombie-like
or gone home and married the bed.

"Our car is one big disaster!"
I warn Camille, as Mom's car *finally* coughs up
to the curb, with a tired sticker
*Math: It's Easy as Pi!*
peeling from the back window.

I cringe—
"It needs to be washed,
and painted,
and then sold!"

"Like I care," scoffs Camille
as she swings open the squeaky door
and smiles at Mom:
        "Hello, Mrs. Wood!"

"Hello, Camille."

        In the shoe shop, Mom holds up
shiny shoes with small stacked heels.
Camille giggles,
and I roll my eyes at Mom.

"What? They're cute," she tries.

"Cute, if you're Sheila," I reply.

"Or Ange," Camille adds.

"Fine, you two choose"
—and she gives up
                too easily
                        and walks away too quickly.

Camille points to a pair
of blue low-top sneakers.

"My thoughts exactly," I say and try them on,
then bring them up to Mom,
who's waiting at the counter to pay.

After the transaction,
Mom snaps her wallet shut
like an exclamation,
        and I wonder if she's angry
or if I've hurt her
somehow.


On the way to the food court,
I sneak peeks at my new shoes
and then at Mom
                who walks out in front of us.
Her shoulders are stiff,
and I can tell
        she's disappointed
        or sad
or something more.


Camille and I order pizza and Sprites
and sit

        at a table
                for two.


Mom positions herself nearby.

I glance over,
        wonder if I'm a good daughter.

She's studying two women
      who are walking and chatting,
arm in arm,
    and then *I know—*


      *She misses Aunt Rose.*


    I have no clue
        what it's like to have a sister,
        much less to lose one.


She looks away from the women
and forces a smile my way,
then tips her slice of pizza at me.


I could go to her
    tell her a joke
        or give her a hug,
          tell her she's a good mom.


"Earth to Abbey!" Camille sings out,
and I'm pulled back
to my friend and our food
in the food court.


"So . . . about Mr. Lydon . . ." Camille begins,
"*you* think he's cute, right?"


"He's our *teacher*, Camille!
And seriously old—like thirty or something!"

"Yeah, but—?"

"Okay, okay . . . I like what he says about art."

"*Sure* you do!"

"I do!
Well, what about *Jacob* and *YOU*?" I tease.

"You know he's just my friend. Besides, I remember when *Jakie*
still slept with a teddy!
Anyway, *he* likes *you*!"

"*Me*?
          Wait—did you say *Jakie*?"

"Yes.
And yes—
*YOU*."


*7*0.

Camille must be wrong.

Here's what I'm used to being:
          the last to be picked,
          that girl over there,
          the one hiding behind her hair,
          counted absent when present,

the one who eats alone,
sits alone,
the quiet type,
a sit-on-the-sidelines type,
the girl who draws,

and lately
*Army brat.*

I lie on my bed tossing Mr. Poodle
up to the ceiling
and trying to catch him
as he
falls
back
down.

*Jacob knows my name.*

*AND*

*Maybe He Likes ME!*

Until that moment,
I'd never noticed
what an awesome canvas
my ceiling would make.
And I decide to paint it,
even if this house is temporary

and I have to move again
soon.


## 71.

Mr. Lydon displays a painting,
and quizzes us:

> "What was Picasso trying to accomplish?
> &
> What do you think blue meant to him?"

I know
          but stare at the blank paper on my table.

"That he was cold!" Sheila laughs.
"Loneliness?" Camille suggests.
"Sadness," Jiman adds.

I look up
and then at Mr. Lydon,
who smiles and says,
"Excellent."

So we begin our monochromatic paintings,
and I choose blue,
               like Picasso.

While painting,
I think of Dad on the base
with the other soldiers
and imagine them discussing camouflage—
its shades of greens, browns, and tans,
and how these colors make them feel.

    He would explain to me, "See, Abbey, in the Army,
    colors have purposes,
    not emotions."

I laugh out loud at this.

Camille grins, surprised to hear my voice in class.

"Inside joke, Abbey?" Mr. Lydon asks.

"Um . . . yeah,"
I squeak.

## 72.

That night,
Dad holds a soft conversation
with the phone—
    *Perhaps it's Uncle Todd?*
But I swear I hear him say,
right before hanging up,

"I love ya, man."

I whip my head
and body toward him,
almost knock my glass
from the table, and demand,

"*Who*    was    that?"

Dad doesn't share
his emotions easily
and keeps his heart
locked up safely.

"Your uncle,"

he says calmly
and comes over and stands
just behind my chair
and almost touches me.

Mom washes our dishes
with her back to us.
I can tell she's crying,
and I think I know
what she's feeling
just from the angle of her head—
and because
she's my mom.

She's thinking
that Dad has to say certain things
before he leaves
just in case he doesn't get the chance
to say them
again.

## 73.

Lately,
Dad busies himself around the house
when he's here:
      changing smoke-detector batteries,
      unclogging gutters,
      checking the oil in the cars,
crossing off items
on some master list
one by one.
And
I wonder . . .
      if I'm on there.

Mostly he's on the base
training—I guess—
for war.

74.

In the cafeteria,
Sheila, Angela, and Lana
surround something, circling like buzzards,
something or *someone*,
with red hair.

*It is Camille.*

I pause for only a second,
then hear them chanting:

"JACOB and CAMILLE!
Better take a pill!"

"He's only a friend!" she growls,
standing up quickly from her chair.
The girls jump back,
startled but cool,
and laugh at Camille,
red-faced and unbalanced.

"You do like *boys*, don't you?"
Lana provokes. And for once,
Camille has no comeback.
I can almost hear Dad in my head:
"Everyone has an Achilles' heel."

And I'm surprised
that the strongest girl I know
has a breaking point.
She is suddenly
    silent,
    un-
    nerved.
    un-
    Camilled.

I push through them
and grab my friend by the hand.
    "It's called a joke," Angela smirks,
but I pull Camille away
and toward the gym,
into her zone, where even
if Tommy says, "You shoot like a girl!"
it's a compliment
when you see Camille
handle
the ball.


75.

On the way home,
Camille is not Camille:
Staring. Quiet. Still.

I give her space
but eventually ask,
"Are you okay?"

"It's just . . .
everyone around here
makes a big freaking deal
out of ev-e-ry-thing!"

"I know."

"Just because two people play ball together—
it doesn't mean *anything* at all.
We're friends!"

"I know."

Camille glares out
the bus's window, at the same houses
we pass every day.

"You know what's cool about you, Abbey?"

"Please tell me," I say seriously.

"You get to be
whoever you want to be in this town.
You're free. No history.

I have to be
      who everyone *expects* me to be.
*Good old Camille.*"

"You think I'm free?" I smirk.
"Free and forever
the newbie, maybe."

"One day, Abbey,
I'll be in college somewhere, far from here,
playing basketball."

"That's funny—you want to leave,
and all *I* want is to stay put," I say
without a smile on my face.

"Yeah, funny," Camille agrees.
"It's a wonder we met at all."


## 76.

The community center oozes orange
and black. Tables overflow with candy,
popcorn, and caramel apples.

Parents are throwing us
a Halloween party,
*Ghouls After School,*

since we're "too old
for trick or treat."

We've been warned to take it easy
on the gore. "Out of respect
for all that's happened."

Mr. Lydon's band, The Hiccups,
plays in a corner. Tommy and Sheila
show their fangs and slow dance.

Angela and Lana float over angelically
to Jacob and me, where we're drinking punch sheepishly,
waiting for Camille to show up.

My costume consists of a shirt
splattered with paint, and Jacob wears
an orange tee with the word
*Costume* written on it.

"What're you *supposed* to be?" Angela stops near me to stare.

"A Jackson Pollock painting," I reply.

"I knew it!" Jacob smiles.

"O-kay." Angela nudges Lana and rolls her eyes, then says,
"Camille must've lost her jockstrap."

I don't say anything,
and neither does Jacob—at first.

*Some friends we are!*

Then suddenly Jacob speaks up,
"Were they all out of pitchforks and horns at The Devil Store?"

Angela and Lana groan
and flutter away. I let a laugh
escape once they're gone.

Then—all in one breath—Jacob describes
a Pollock-inspired project he once made
and how he mostly plays soccer now
but his favorite teacher was Mr. Lydon last year
and *do I like Mr. Lydon, too?*

"He's definitely my favorite!" I agree,
and a new kind of warmth floods me.

Jacob grins back,
and we glance once more
toward the door,
waiting for our shared friend
to appear.

When Camille finally shows,
clad in jersey and high-tops,

I'm annoyed that Angela
got the gist of her costume right.

Feeling the need to say
*I'm sorry*
     or
     *I'm a loser friend*
for not defending her,
I push Jacob in Camille's direction
and we rush over to her.

     Then the three of us
spend most of the night
huddled around a bowl of candy,
laughing and eating
only the good chocolates
and voting on our
all-time favorite
costumes.

## 11.

After the dance, I wait at the curb
for Mom to show up.

I'm beginning to think she forgot
since Jacob and Camille
and most of the others have left.

Mr. Lydon, loading instruments,
calls to me: "You okay, Abbey?"
"Yeah," I say, before spying
Angela and Lana approaching
with arms full of dismantled decor.

"Waiting on Mommy?" they giggle
but don't stop for my reaction
       because they've spotted what looks like
Jiman and a little boy
walking by themselves,
her arm tight around
his shoulder.

"Who invited *you*?!" Angela yells.
"Ange!" Lana claps her hand over Angela's mouth,
"You're so mean!"
       But the expression
on Jiman's face doesn't seem to change,
although I'm too far away to tell for sure.

What I don't do
is tell them to shut up,
to leave people alone for once
because mostly I'm relieved
that they've forgotten
about me.

78.

Most afternoons,
I find Mom lying on her bed
with books propped around her
neither sleeping
nor reading.

Once a week, she writes
a letter to Jackson and Kate
from our kitchen table
and asks me to draw
a "happy" picture on it.

One time, I sketch
a pink flower blooming
up the side of the paper—
and for some reason,
this makes her cry
and lock herself
in her bedroom
for the weekend.

79.

Does someone stay the age
they die forever? A still life,

a photograph, a timeline
stopped, a forever blank spot
in their family's future?

I dream Aunt Rose
takes an elevator skyward,
finger on the *Up* button,
Willy Wonka style,
zipping like a shooting star
across New York's horizon.

I hope
the rivers run chocolate
where she is. And they have music.
And *all* the instruments.
And a twinkling of souls
strung 'round the dark
like a party where she's
the honored guest
all dressed
in light.

Mom hopes,
she whispers in a broken voice,
"One day they find her
or some of her bones,
find something to lay beneath
the ground and a stone
we can write her name on."

## 80.

Camille tells me
that Jacob informed her
that Sheila's boyfriend Tommy
and some eighth-graders
were caught after hours
at the elementary school next door
throwing rocks at a little boy
and calling him "Terrorist!"
because of his name
and the shade of his skin.

I recall
Dad's words:
"It's what they do.
They're terrorists."

*But*

   *He's just a little boy!*

## 81.

  In the cafeteria,
I overhear some girls at a table nearby
gossiping and pointing in Jiman's direction.

Jiman sketches in a sketchbook.

*Does she know they're talking about her?*

Any other day,
they could be
just as easily
talking about me.

I hear
them say
that she moved here
from somewhere up north,
or maybe farther away,
that her parents run a restaurant in town.
>*Who'd eat there!*
>the girls laugh
and
>*Terrorists!*
>they whisper.

But I am thinking:
*My parents and I will.*
*We*
*will*
*eat there.*

## 82.

Today
for the first time ever,

Jiman doesn't sit alone on the bus.
She sits with a little boy,
who usually sits near the driver.
Perhaps he's her brother.
He looks like the boy from Halloween.
I wonder if he's the ONE
they threw rocks at.

Jiman sits on the outside
facing the aisle, as if daring
anyone to bother them,
and the little boy sits by the window.
He crouches low in the seat
and pretends to sleep.

83.

We're having class outdoors.
I zip my jacket from the autumn chill.

Mr. Lydon has instructed us
to pick a "natural" object to draw.
So I wander around, begin sketching
a large rock that lies left of the soccer field,
a rock kids hang out on after school.
        But I crumple my page, move on.

I come to Aunt Rose's tree,

the one I tied a ribbon around in September,
and I sit at its base.

The branches are mostly empty now.
Like arms, they could hug me
if they could bend.

Dry leaves surround the tree—
like clothing fallen free.
I think of Dad's camouflage
and its shades of color
meant to keep him hidden.

A few branches have broken and are hanging crooked,
from where kids must have swung from them.

It's a lovely tree, really.

After sketching it,
I re-tie the faded ribbon
and think of Aunt Rose,
before leaving
to look for
Camille.


84.

It's *that* time again.

"Has your monthly visitor come to call?" Mom asks,
which seriously irritates me
because a visitor should be invited
or wanted, or at least have permission
to drop by.

       I spend lots of time
in the bathroom and my bedroom,
crossing off the days
until my "company" departs.

At least this time,
Mom caves and writes an excuse for P.E.
that lets me sit out, lean against the wall
and draw, try to avoid the stray basketballs
that always seem to find me. But I regret
leaving Camille alone in the locker room,
so each time she looks my way from the court,
I wave or give her a thumbs-up
for the points she scores.

       Tommy asks her to play H-O-R-S-E,
so The Trio
cheer loudly on the sidelines for Tommy—
but mostly Sheila boos Camille,
who makes shot
after
glorious
shot!

85.

All week long,
Mom lets me order
my takeout favorites—
enchiladas, pizza, lo mein—
says she's lost the energy to cook.
I make heaping plates for Dad
and leave them wrapped up
in the fridge.

Before bed each night,
I warm a heating pad
filled with starchy-smelling rice
and sleep curled around it,
like I used to sleep
with Mr. Poodle.

In the mornings,
the heating pad has slipped
between the wall and the bed,
and the plates for Dad
are scraped clean and waiting
in the sink.

86.

Mom and I hang out
mostly without talking these days.

We speak an unspoken language,
a mother-daughter language
that leaves a lot open
to interpretation.
I mention my art class
in case she might want to ask
about it, but she's listening
to news on the radio
while pushing her noodles
around with chopsticks,
so I sketch her face,
between bites.

Words on the radio are tossed about,
words like *hijackers* and *evil-doers*.

I want to talk about Aunt Rose.

But Mom shrugs:
        "I can't talk about that right now."


## 87.

Camille has a dentist appointment
so I'm alone on the bus again—
not really alone—
but sometimes
it feels that way

with lots of people around,
people who don't really know me,
listening
and witnessing
what goes down.

The football boys perch
a few rows back.
And I will them
not to target me,
especially since Jacob
is within hearing
range today.

Jiman boards the bus,
passes the little boy, who might be her brother,
and heads toward the middle, toward us.
Others deliberately scoot their backpacks over
to take up their half-empty seats.
She pauses briefly near me.
Unfortunately, I look up too late,
drop my sketchpad, watch my pencils roll away.
Jacob stifles a giggle, whispers,
"Awk-ward!" and waits
for me to agree.

Then I surprise myself
and him
when I whip around

and snap, "Shut up!
She might hear you."

Stunned or hurt, he says,

           "I was kidding
                and talking
                    about *you,*
      *Abbey,*" and hands me
      a handful
      of runaway
      colored

      pencils.

88.

It's Saturday night
and we're trying out a new restaurant,
one of our long-standing Wood family traditions
for when we're celebrating.
Tonight, it's my choice
so I choose Middle Eastern food,
hoping the place might belong to Jiman's family.

*What would I say if I happened to see her?*

"So what's the occasion?" I ask my parents
       between bites of savory rice.

Mom and Dad exchange worry.

    *"What?"* I brace myself
for what I'm about to feel.

Like a balloon losing its air,
Dad starts to explain,

"Very soon . . .
    I'm going . . .
        to be leaving . . .
            for Afghanistan."

"Wh-When?" I ask, confused,

    and, "For how long?"

"We knew this was coming, remember?
I warned you.
Maybe a six-month tour."

"You didn't say *Afghanistan*!"

"Well, I didn't know then, but now it's clear.
It's my job, Abbey, it's what I *do*."

"Can't you *do* anything else?"

*because*

*what if . . .*
*something terrible*
*happens*
*over*
*there?*

I push back
      from the table
just as the waiter reaches over
to refill my water,
and I knock the pitcher
           out of his hand.

He apologizes like it was his fault,
      as I stare blankly back at him.

"Abbey," Dad says gently,
and mops the table with his napkin.

"Abbey," he says again,

      and suddenly I'm filled
with fear—

      but for whom or what
           I don't know.

      And that's when I see Jiman
and the little boy,

who has to be her brother,
smiling from a picture
behind the cash register.

*I chose the right restaurant!*

Beneath their picture,
a plaque reads
FOOD, FAMILY, AND FRIENDS.
And I repeat those words to myself
again and again until
I am calm.

89.

The details are vague,
so Dad packs his gear
and polishes various pieces
of equipment each night.
His rucksack stays bloated
by the door, as we
await his orders.

Each morning, he reports
to the base earlier than usual,
trains all day, then returns to our house
in the dark. The specifics
of his deployment are one

BIG secret, so we act
like nothing is different.

Sometimes it feels
like we're pretending,
like we're dolls in a dollhouse,
just waiting, in whatever position
we've been placed.

Here's what we look like:
      Mom sits at the kitchen table,
      arms bent, math papers
      in front of her. I sit at my desk,
      head forward, notebook
      open like I'm studying,
      and Dad sits in the reclining chair,
      holding a paper,
      dozing.

But I want to shout at them, startle them from their positions:

*Wake up, Woods!*

*What if something happens?*

      *What then?*

## 90.

But we go on
with our family routines.

For a few days now after school,
Mom's been changing from her teaching clothes
to cook a vegetable or a dessert.

It keeps her mind off Aunt Rose
and Dad's deployment.

"There will be eight of us," she says, trying to smile.
"A full house for Thanksgiving!"
But Dad reminds her
        he may be "in and out."

She's making a turkey *and* a ham.

"Rose always has—
        *had* both at her house," she explains.

I peel the sweet potatoes,
studying Jackson and Kate
in their school pictures on the fridge.
Aunt Rose's MISSING flyer
has gone missing, and I look at Mom
stirring gravy on the stove.

        What's it like for my cousins?

I haven't seen them
since the memorial.

This will be their first Thanksgiving
at *our* house. Their first Thanksgiving
without their mom.

What will they give thanks for?
They have given so much.

## 91.

I search my room
for things I've outgrown—
clothes, chapter books, small toys—
to hand
      down to Kate.
Mom said she'd help me,
but she must be preoccupied
with food prep.

Each year,
we pass along
things I no longer need.
This year,
nothing I own
seems good
enough.

Kate and Aunt Rose always go through it all
like it's Christmas,
with Aunt Rose saying things like,
"Katie, you'll look so pretty in this,"
and, "We love your hand-me-downs, Abbey.
Every piece has a story!"


One time, Kate tried on a yellow coat,
too big still, but in the pocket
she found a tiny stuffed kitten.
      "Can I keep him? Please!
      I'll name him Larry,"
      she'd squealed, and we'd laughed
and laughed and rolled on the floor.


      Since then, Kate always checks
the pockets of my clothes first.
And sometimes I leave surprises
in them for her to find.


Before she was born,
      when it was just Jackson and me,
I remember us once being propped
on either side of a seesaw, Mom behind Jackson
for some reason, and Aunt Rose behind me.
We balanced perfectly,
and when Mom and Aunt Rose
stepped away from us
we just hung there
suspended in the air,

our chubby legs kicking,
and all of us giggling
at our miraculous
feat.


## 92.

I give extra THANKS
for a few days out of school.
But even away from it all,
I hear the boys on the bus,
their insults flying,
visualize The Trio
eyeballing.


*It's just a little name-calling,*
Dad would coach me.
*Toughen Up!*


It could be worse.
No one's throwing rocks at me.


I think of Jiman.
And her little brother.
Her parents and their restaurant,
and I'm thankful for them,
thankful that they
moved here too.

## 93.

My relatives arrive wrinkled and dazed
in late afternoon. Uncle Todd bursts
into our house with multiple boxes in his hands
and stacks them on our kitchen table.
Jackson and Kate follow him,
                                    and we all
hang around the edges of the room
with hands shoved in pockets or folded
across chests, staring, watching him
tear into boxes as if he must get this done
before he can unpack his suitcase and settle in.
            Mom pours apple ciders and passes the cups
around. Uncle Todd pulls crumpled newspapers
from the boxes and uncovers a violin
and gives it to Mom, who holds it like a baby.
He unwraps a pair of painted maracas,
stares at them for a second, then hands them to me.
I shake them softly, recalling how Aunt Rose
taught me to hold them so the sound resonated
and was not muted or dulled by my hands.
            Jackson abruptly leaves the room, his shoulder
brushing the doorframe, his shoes screeching
a discordant note in retreat.
            Kate stands frozen, eyes darting from face to face.

After two whole beats of silence, Uncle Todd
clears his throat and tells Mom,
"She would've wanted you to have them."

"Thank you," Mom whispers,
tears brimming her eyes.

Then Uncle Todd pulls Kate toward him
and pries her arms loose from across her chest.
She smiles and complains, "Quit it, Dad!"
Which makes me think of *my* dad,
who is on the base,
but will be leaving
soon.

94.

Jackson stares out our windows,
hands safe in his pockets.

*What* does he see out there?

The wind is blowing,
branches sway,
a few birds flit
from leafless tree
to tree.

He seems to be looking beyond these.

I try to think of something to say.

"You want to go outside?"

but maybe
he doesn't hear me,
      or maybe
I don't really say it.


## 95.

Jackson, Kate, and I
sit on the porch in the chilly fall air, waiting
for Thanksgiving to begin.

So much has happened to *me* this year
but even more to *them*.

When Grandma Jill and Grandpa Paul arrive,
they bring smiles and hugs and good ideas.

Before Grandpa has even unloaded their car,
Grandma proclaims:

"Let's start a tradition—a banner for Thanksgiving!"

Grandpa chuckles and brings in a roll
of paper and a box of markers from their trunk.

The grown-ups sit by the fire and watch us in silence.

Jackson writes the words,

Kate colors them in,
and I draw a cartoon turkey.

We string the banner across the dining room.

Little by little, as we're eating,
      it slopes
            downward
                  toward
                        our Thanksgiving dinner,
then suddenly—
            dips into
                  the sweet potatoes.

We all laugh until
      Kate tips backward out of her chair
            and Jackson snorts tea from his nose,
then we all laugh some more.

After dinner, I overhear Uncle Todd
say to Mom and Grandma in the kitchen,
"They're okay, but Jackson's acting up
at school."
            He pauses, then continues,
"It's just good to see them being kids."

## 96.

At bedtime, Grandpa tells a story
about Mom and Aunt Rose
and the day they learned to ride
their matching Christmas bikes.

With the image of them in my head
as little girls,
I cut a smile toward Uncle Todd,
then quickly look away
when I glimpse his broken heart.

Grandpa tells the story as if nothing has changed.
He tells the story as if we've all *agreed*
to talk about Aunt Rose.
He tells the story,
and we listen,
piled up and overlapping
on the couch,
where Jackson will sleep,
and on the air mattress,
where Uncle Todd and Kate will sleep.

    Just last summer
    Kate begged Aunt Rose
    to let her sleep with me
    in my "big girl" bed.

As Grandpa's story
comes to an end,
and we're supposed to laugh
about how they both refused to use
training wheels,
everyone just smiles, tears streaking
most of our faces.

We say
our good nights and go
our own ways, but Kate
doesn't follow me this year
to my room.
And I guess I feel relieved;
her sadness
is so huge.

      Soon, the house is full
of quiet, sleeping noise.

Aunt Rose's voice
          was the one voice missing
                 from our evening.

But I'm glad Grandpa talked about her—
out loud
in our house.

## 97.

In the morning,
Mom and Grandma are banging pans
around in the kitchen. The smell
of bacon and coffee stirs me.
I toss in my bed, thinking how Dad
will be leaving any day now,
how I could be like
Jackson and Kate,
and wondering

> *if Aunt Rose seems* gone *to them*
*or like*
> *she'll return home soon.*

I leave my bed
and find *both* my cousins
still asleep.
Jackson has joined Kate
on the air mattress,
his arm thrown across her back.
Uncle Todd must be
the one in the shower.
For a few minutes, I watch
them sleep, check
for peeking eyes.
They look like babies—
soft and happy.

Then someone shuffles around upstairs,
     and for a fraction of a second
     Dad crosses my mind
     . . . and the possibility
of the unthinkable
happening.

Then suddenly,
I want to wake Jackson and Kate
and tell them I love them,

        but I tiptoe past instead.

98.

Our holiday comes to an end,
and we hug and say our goodbyes.

     Then,
     without warning,
     Uncle Todd begins to cry.

Jackson and Kate just stare,
their arms hanging loose at their sides.
Grandpa gives him a bear hug.

My uncle looks at Dad,
and then at me,
and says,

"Abbey, your dad is one good man!
Rose would be so proud."

I'm not sure what he means
or why he says this now,
but I smile at him
like Abbey Fabulous would,
and he hugs me tightly
around the head.

## 99.

The President
of the United States
has come to town
        to tour the base.

It's all over the news—
        and Dad's busier than usual.

In the few minutes he's actually home,
he explains, "It's because we're about to go."

And by "go" I know what he means,

but I try to connect these events:

*Dad leaving*

and

*the president arriving*

like a cause-and-effect sentence
                    or a dot-to-dot that reveals an image,
yet the lines aren't straight and people disagree about the big picture.
Like Camille's dad, who's protesting
the president's visit.


100.

During the holidays,
Dad and I always split a wishbone,
a tradition of ours.
Mom locates it, washes it,
and then dries it on the kitchen
windowsill.

Usually I wish

*to become a world-famous artist*

because I usually break off
the biggest piece—
or maybe Dad lets me win.


This year, before bedtime,

he comes into my bedroom
"Hey there, Abbey the Artist!"
and holds up the wishbone.

"You wanna?"

And, of course,
      I break off the winning piece.

But I don't feel like a winner
and I'm torn this year
      between
            making a wish for Jackson and Kate
            and making a wish for him.

# DECEMBER

101.

With Thanksgiving over,
  we search for *Afghanistan*
    on the Internet.


It's not where
I thought it was.
One map calculates
the exact distance in miles
that will separate Dad from us,
and it's over seven thousand.
I speculate that most
of my classmates
could not locate Afghanistan
or even spell it
correctly.


  Dad traces his flight route
on the monitor with a steady finger
so Mom can know
where they will lay over.


I place my finger on Tennessee,
the place where we currently sleep,
and notice how it looks like an arrow pointing elsewhere.

*Is this state really my home?*

I study the blue expanse of water
that Dad will cross,
and then
        stab my finger
on the place
where he will sleep and work
for a while.

"We can write each other . . .
        . . . and talk occasionally,"
he offers softly.

"Yeah," I whisper.

But when I ask,
"What will you be doing there?"

He stammers
        like he doesn't really know
        or doesn't want to tell me.


## 102.

Camille's absent
so I sit alone at lunch, hyperaware
of every little stare and the cafeteria filling up around me—

until Angela, Sheila, and Lana
commandeer my table,
open their lunches, and spread out
their yogurts, carrots, and pretzels.

*Surrounded!*

I don't know how I feel about this.
There are so many of them.

*Do they like me now?*

I can't help myself
and start to sweat, look around to see who notices
the infamous three
sitting with me.

"So . . ." Sheila begins casually
        but with the hint of an agenda,
                "where's Camille?"

I choke down a bite
of PB&honey,
and quickly spit out her whereabouts: "At home."

"And what's with this little getup?" Angela
points to my plaid shirt,
jeans, and painted high-tops.
I search my brain

for something cool
or witty to say.

Then Sheila nudges Lana,
who asks, as if she's rehearsed it,
"So. We really need to know—
does Camille like Tommy

or what?"

A small part of me wants The Trio
to stay,

but then Dad comes to mind
and how he talks about *duty*,

about *doing the right thing*.

So I just shrug.
"You'd have to ask Camille."

The Trio's disappointment is visible.
They can't pack up their lunches
fast enough.

## 103.

Later,
in Ms. Dequire's room—
the one class with a seating chart—
I sit beside Lana, who rolls her eyes,

scoots her desk a little farther from mine,
and turns her chair so her back is to me.
At one point, she coughs and chokes
and complains to anyone nearby,
"What's that god-awful
smell?"


## 104.

Afternoons
at our house,
Mom nails the role
of merry parent, singing out loud
like a Dickens caroler:
"This shall be a holiday to remember!
A Christmas of firsts for the Woods!"
She instructs me, "Chin up. Be joyful!"
her finger poking the air
for emphasis.

So we try new things—
or the things Dad usually does
when he's not too busy with work—
like building fires,
shopping for a Christmas tree,
and stringing lights around our house.
Mom works extra hard
to appear convincingly
spirited.

It's almost like Dad's gone already
since he's on the base
practically full time now.

In the cold night air
when he finally gets home,
we stand back in the yard
to admire the twinkling lights
that I've wound around
the porch columns.
And I can sense he's impressed,
but I need him this once
just to say it.


## 105.

Mom
goes overboard,
trying to make Christmas perfect,
doling out
present after present
like a crazed elf.

My loot piles up,
and my stocking spills over
with chocolates,
colored pencils,
and paintbrushes.

Dad gives us
personalized canisters of Mace,
tied with decorative
red ribbons.

"How romantic!" Mom laughs
and plants a kiss on his cheek.

He also pulls
from behind his back
a stuffed pink poodle,
just like my purple one,
except this one is sporting
Army fatigues, and he
tosses it
lovingly
to me.

Big surprise—I miss!

A stuffed dog and Mace!

> *He must be trying to decide*
> *if I'm a teenager yet or not.*

To Mom, I give a picture
I've drawn of Dad and her
on the beach.

For Dad, I've made a calendar
with themed artwork for each month.
I'm most proud of January.

"You can cross off the days," I explain.

"It's amazing!" he begins,
          "but I hate to bring it with me—
in case something happens . . .

          "—to it," he adds quickly.

"But you *have* to take it!" I practically whimper.

"Sweetie, your dad *loves* it," Mom reassures,
misunderstanding me
or the moment.

## 106.

Later,
to spread some joy,
I call Camille
and chuckle
"Ho! Ho! Ho!"
into the receiver.

"Ab-bey! I thought you were a perv!"

We get down to talking presents—
my set of paints and brushes,
her collectible basketball jersey—
and we schedule a movie date.

Then
like she can read my mind
and knows I'm worried about Jacob
because I snapped at him
that day on the bus,
she says,

"I can bring Jakie
            as my gift to you!"

and we conclude our Christmas call
            all giggles
                    and silly goodbyes.


107.

Then,
like any other Wednesday,
the day Dad departs arrives.
We're military. We should be
prepared for this.

Dad heads to the base
before the sun begins to rise.

Mom and I delay at home,
eating bowls of loud cereal.
Mom mostly stares at hers.

The hangar on the base
is draped in red, white, and blue,
and a soldier plays the trumpet.
I spy a few kids who look familiar.

Families crowd the bleachers.
Several babies are crying
and young children yawning.
The soldiers look exactly alike
with varying heights
when they march in and file
into the neat rows of chairs.
As always, I'm confused at first
by the perfect sameness
of their uniforms and movements.
I sway forward on the bleachers
and close my eyes for a moment,
then spot Dad when he stands
and walks to the podium to say
some official words. Mom motions
to him and grabs my hand—

and I don't pull it away.

Finally, we all wave the small flags
someone has passed out to us.

For what seems like only seconds,
the camouflaged soldiers break away
from their rows—and we locate Dad
and hold onto him.

       I don't know what
words we say, but tears affect my vision,
and Mom wipes her nose with a tissue.
Then, in no time, he returns
to the formation, and they march
          from the room
            and out onto the tarmac.

In a big crying crowd, we follow
and watch the plane open up.

One by one
soldiers begin to disappear—

                      and then Dad is gone,

and I wish
I could've thought more clearly
or placed something special—
like a good luck charm or our latest wishbone—
in his hand, or hugged him harder,
or told him I loved him.

*Did I forget*
*to tell him*
*that?*

## 108.

Two words. Maybe it was a phrase?

     *B positive*

almost like a message to someone, like a secret code,
almost like something I imagined he whispered,
almost like a bumper sticker or Army slogan
or strange jargon

painted on Dad's combat boots.

*B positive*

I know I saw it.
There's no mistaking it.
*I'm not making it up.*

So I ask Mom.
And she cracks the code.

"His blood type," she laughs
hysterical-like, as if she's just revealed
the punch line of a joke.

Through a forced grin, she adds,
"At least we had Christmas together!"

"His blood type on his shoes?"
I fail to comprehend.

Perhaps he wrote it
so I would see it as he walked away.

Was it an omen?

No, the very sound of it is uplifting:

*B positive*

*B positive*

*B positive*

"That's your blood type, too,"
Mom tells me,
pulling me from
my stupor.

# JANUARY

109.

"Happy 2002!"
> —Mom and I hug each other
>> as the ball drops
>>> in Times Square.

We clink fizzy drinks
and zone out to the TV—

Jackson, Kate,
Uncle Todd, and Dad
crowd our sleepy minds.

"New York is picking itself back up." Mom sighs.

Then we settle
into the couch,
under a blanket we share,
where we'll sleep into the light
of a brand-new year.
I'm in Mom's arms,
like when I was little,
and as I drift off,
I whisper

*Goodbye*

in my head
or maybe out loud
     to 2001
     and tick off the year's life-changing events:

the year we moved to Tennessee,
the year of the terrorist attacks,
the year my period arrived,
the year Aunt Rose died,
and the year Dad left for Afghanistan.

When I wake,
Mom and the magic of the night
are gone.

## 110.

Back to school.
And Mom is busy, busy, busy—
always grading or lesson planning,
taking deliberate, controlled breaths,
flipping from news station to news station
(as if she'll catch a glimpse of Dad
on the TV war), stirring
a cup of tea, or repetitively
checking her e-mail.

I thought we'd talk more
     with just the two of us here.

But it's the opposite,
which is okay by me,
for now,
I guess.


## 111.

*Dear Dad,*

*Mom misses you. She's still super sad about Aunt Rose.*
*She talks on the phone a ton to Uncle Todd, Grandma*
*and Grandpa, and Gram & Gramps.*

*They all miss you, too!*

*In Art, I'm creating a monochromatic painting.*
*Mono means one, as in one main color.*
*When it's done, I can send it to you.*

*Come home soon.*

*Your monodaughter,*

*Abbey*


## 112.

I doodle on the corner of the letter I've written.

*Did it actually happen?*
*Did buildings really fall?*
*Or was it just a scene*
*from a movie I once saw?*

Without witnessing something firsthand,
it's hard to believe in it after a while—
the way it's hard to believe that someone you know
is no longer living, breathing,
and being.

But if buildings as grand as those
can just vanish . . . it must be so.

Sometimes, our life with Aunt Rose
feels imagined
like I never really knew her at all.

I try to remember her easy laugh,
her singing voice,
picture her face—
or maybe the face I recall
is her photo face from the flyer we made.
I try to bring tears to my eyes,

but I can't anymore.

Then there's Dad
in Afghanistan.

It's hard to envision him there.

Maybe that *tree falling* saying is true.

*If a tree falls in a forest and no one is around to hear it,*
*does it make a sound?*

Although I might revise it:

*If your father gets killed in a war and he's half a map from you,*
*would you believe that he's gone?*

I don't know what

                        to believe in anymore.


## 113.

A few days ago, my mom and I
stopped at a grocery store near the base,
and all the way down a bright aisle,
way down near the cereal,
we thought we saw Dad, but *he*
was just some other kid's military dad.

## 114.

He's left us before,
                        for many months at a time,
but he's never been this far away,
or maybe I was too young to know.


The house has grown quiet
without him, without his fatherly voice,
his boots by the door, his steady presence
moving through the house, the creaks
and groans and closings of doors
that are distinctly his. Until now,
I've never realized how each of us
makes our own unique sounds doing the same things—
like washing our hands or shutting a drawer.


His clothes hang motionless in his closet.
His pillow is unmoved.
His books lie dusty and unread by the bed.
His coffee cup is always clean
and in its place in the cabinet.
His aftershave is full, full, full—
            so just once,
            I dab it on my neck.


*I didn't realize I would miss him like this.*


Maybe it's because Mom isn't actually HERE.
She's just putting on clothes each day,

pretending.
She hasn't been anywhere really
since Aunt Rose.


## 115.

Camille's family
hangs a hand-painted flag
of peace signs and doves
across their front door:
MAKE LOVE NOT WAR.
I cringe at the words, stare
dumbly at the doorbell
forever and a day, deciding
if Dad stands for one
more than the other.
And if they're against the war,
does that make them against
Dad? Against me?
Can you support one
but not the other?
But what I really can't figure
is if I'm not welcome
at Camille's house
anymore.

## 116.

The mailbox sits cold and empty,
bored and unfriendly.

Dad said it would take a while
for his platoon to get set up,
for him to be able to correspond.

Mom checks the mail
even more often than I do.

From two blocks away,
the mailman sees us coming
and nods his official nod
and looks the other way.

We're not upset with *him*.


## 117.

Jacob must have forgiven me
for snapping at him that day on the bus
because he and Camille slip happy notes
into my locker and try to crack me up
by dancing and goofing off in the halls.
I laugh, despite myself, and forget—
for a few moments—about the war.

## 118.

Then finally—

*A letter!*

A letter from Dad arrives!

## 119.

The battered envelope
smells of faraway places
and contains a page for me
and a page for Mom.

She holds hers close all day
and falls asleep with it—

Dad's words
beneath her pillow.

## 120.

*Dear Abbey,*

*I hope school is mono-derful (get it—one-derful?)*
*and that you're making some new friends.*
*Tell Camille I say hello.*

*We're settling in, but communication*
*may be difficult at times.*

*I'm picturing your painting in my head right now.*
*The landscape here is monochromatic.*

*I think about you and Mom every day.*

*Miss you.*

*Love,*
*Dad*

## 121.

Mom has joined a "support group."

*It's her New Year's resolution.*

Over dinner, she briefly explains:
    "I had a sister and she died . . .
        and I have to deal with that."

"But you *are* dealing with it,"
I insist, searching her face.
    "*We* are dealing, right?"

She looks down at her plate.
"If I could've said goodbye
or seen her again, it would've
been different, I think."

Later, after brushing her teeth,
she adds, "Plus, it'll help me
be stronger, be a better
mother to you."

I hug her and realize I'm almost
as tall as she is now.

Lying in bed, I decide
on *my* New Year's resolution:

To be a stronger person, too.

I make a mental list of courageous things I could do:

Not care
what The Trio thinks.
Speak up in Art so Mr. Lydon sees I have a brain.
Tell the boys on the bus to stuff it.
Tell Dad I love him the next time we talk.
Be more like Jiman.
Like Camille.
Be brave.
Be strong.

But it's late at night
when so many things
seem possible.

## 122.

I'm learning life goes on,
when someone you love is in Afghanistan.
In a war.

Sometimes the daily chores—
like brushing my teeth,
my hair, going to school,
and eating three meals—
interrupt the hoping
to hear from him.

The waiting is heavy, especially for Mom.
        Between each letter, each call,
we wait to hear from him again,
just the sound of his voice.

        *Aunt Rose's voice is totally gone.*

Sometimes I hear Dad in my head.

Just the little things he says,
like how he jokes
when I flip the channels,

"Whoa! Stop this ride. Let me get off."

123.

The dining room is too big
> and we're saving it for when Dad returns,
> so we eat in the kitchen now.

"What *is* he doing exactly?" I ask.

"They're looking
> for the terrorists who attacked us."

"Is everyone there a terrorist?"

"No, of course not," Mom explains.

"Someone at school said our troops will kill innocent people.
How will they know the good guys from the bad?"

"It's not black and white," she tries.
"It's deeply complicated."

So I just close my eyes, hold my breath, and ask it:
> "He won't get hurt, will he?"

She picks up her plate and walks to the sink,
> stands with her back to me.

"He's good at what he does," she finally states.

Her answer's no good,
and she knows it,
        and I think of Jackson and Kate,
                and how they're a family of three now.

*How do you ever get used*
                        *to a shift like that?*

Even with simple things, like when
my family moves to a new house, *my* brain
gets stuck. In my last bedroom,
I slept beside a window, and even now,
many months later, when I first wake,
I sit up and try to look out the wall.

        All of a sudden it hits me!

                I know exactly what I want
more than being left alone on the bus—
because, face it, I make a good target.

When I think super hard, really concentrate on it,
I don't believe I've ever felt *at home*
in the houses we've lived in
or the schools I've known.

*At home within myself.*
*Like I truly belong.*

## 124.

In Language Arts the next day,
Ms. Johnson instructs us
to compose a letter or a poem,
or a few words to enclose
in a package for one of "our service members."

I look up, surprised by her words—

          I stall, my paper waiting . . .
and steal glances at the kids
               in my class
sitting awkwardly at their small desks.

      Directly in front of me,
      Tommy jots words on his paper,
then nods at another boy
as if to say,
          *Mission Accomplished!*

When Ms. Johnson gathers all of our notes
and folds them into a large envelope,
she walks straight toward me
and places it onto *my* desk.

I stare
like it's a bomb about to go off.
All the other eyes in class
stare at me.

Am I the only *Army brat* in this class?

"Thank your dad for us!" she says kindly,
then moves on, as if checking an item
off a to-do list.

That night, in my room,
I read the notes one by one,
sitting in a circle of my classmates' words:

*Thanks for protecting me!*

*We're so proud of you!*

And from Football Tommy:

*Thanks for keeping my family free!*

I remove one anonymous letter from the stack
that contains only three words,
read it over a few dozen times:

*War is wrong!*

And then shred it
to protect
Dad.


## 125.

Gram & Gramps, Dad's parents,
have traveled from Florida to visit us.
It's Dad's birthday in two weeks
but for some reason they've brought
a present for *me*.

It's large and wrapped in sheets
and tied with an enormous blue bow.

They sleep in the bedroom next to mine,
and their snores are welcome noise
in our hushed-up house.

     Together, we wrap token gifts for Dad
and secure them in a box of foam peanuts,
to which I add the envelope from class
and my monochromatic painting.

During their visit,
we snap photos for him.

In one, I'm opening
the large present
they've brought for me.

I pull away the sheets
            to reveal

                        an easel
fully stocked with oils—
and my mouth is totally gaping.

"It was your father's easel," Gram explains.

"He never told me about this!"

I run my hands all around the frame
and practically want to hug the thing.

In another photo,
Mom wears a birthday hat
and blows Dad a kiss.

In the last one,
Gram & Gramps
look like worried parents
saying the word
"Cheese!"

126.

The walls in this house are thin.

I can hear
Mom and Gram & Gramps in the kitchen.

Mom calls Jackson and Kate
        the "littlest victims of 9/11."

        But they're just my cousins.

Then Gramps says something like
        ". . . and all the military families, too.
The ramifications are huge."

(Note to self: Look up *ramifications*.)

And when they stop talking
as I come in, they don't know
that their silence
is what I fear
the most.

127.

Standing at my locker,
I sense The Trio
coming up from behind,

but it's too quick to consider
*who's going to see*
*and who's going to be*
*their victim du jour.*

As they close in,
I visualize soldiers
and the rhythmic thud of their boots
and the uniform movements of their arms and legs,
and how it's predictable,
because you know what's coming next.

Perhaps they should get credit
for sticking together. Maybe *they* are
"the best they can be" when
they're three.

"Take a picture. It will last longer!" Lana says
as they pass,
and I close my mouth
and then my locker
to follow them
to our classroom.


128.

In Social Studies,
I discover that Angela's brother
has *just* deployed.

My heart feels some
kind of feeling for her.

I consider passing her desk
and saying to her:
"I know how you feel…"
if I could only invoke a braver
version of myself.

Would she look up—
confused at first—then smile
when she realizes how
not all that different we are?

By themselves, each
of The Trio is civil somehow.
It's together that they become
public enemy number one.

## 129.

It's a stay-at-home SNOW day!

Mom moves about the house
        washing sheets, chopping broccoli,
                planning lessons, and writing her daily letter to Dad.

I'm drawing with my colored pencils,
trying to capture *snow*—

I draw . . . erase . . .

        draw . . . erase . . .

               until my hands ache,

    the paper's whiteness intimidating,

blinding—the colors too colorful, the snow not snowy enough.


    I need something, but I don't know what.


A *new* medium maybe?

Different lighting?


    And then suddenly I know!


    *Where's Dad's easel?*


I carry it from the laundry room

           and into our kitchen,

    still in solid disbelief that he ever painted,

attach the paper,

and decide to go with colors—

    a swirling world of colorized snow.


As I paint I decide,

    this one's for Dad,


Then suddenly I stop—


    Three words have been neatly carved into the easel.


I inspect it closely.

Across the top of the frame,
three words
carved intentionally—

> *Who*
> *am*
> *I?*

I trace the letters with my paint-stained finger.
My brush lingers in the air like a question.

                              By the way he's etched
these words into wood,
I think I know *just* how he feels.

*Could this really be*
                    *MY dad?*

Hasn't he always known who he is
and what he wants
with his Army way
of life?


130.

Out of nowhere,
the-one-and-only Sheila appears at my locker.
I assume she's looking for someone behind me,

but she whips out
a cupid-shaped invitation
and hands it to me
and recites:

      "My Valentine's Party—at the Country Club.
      *Everyone's* coming. Not to be missed!"

When she walks away, I stand there
fumbling with my combination,
three times not getting it right.

Then I overhear Lana and Angela in passing:
      "Everyone who's anyone will be there,
        and most of the football and soccer teams."

My heart jumps when I think
of Jacob and me together at a party for Valentine's.
Then—*Voilà!*—my locker opens,
and I feel a rush of success
      that feels like *belonging*, like I'm a part of something,
        and I can't wait
to debrief
with Camille on the bus.

What's more, during class,
      Lana asks what I'll wear,
        and scoots her desk an inch closer to mine,
        and whispers,

      "Jacob will be there!"

131.

On the bus ride home, I'm more confident than ever,
talking a mile a minute.

Then Camille drops the bomb:

"Guess who's NOT invited?

But I'm okay with it," she adds quickly,
"I have other plans. There're hoops
to shoot!" She grins.

"But—but why? I don't get it!" I stutter, my mouth forming an O.
"Why would they invite *me*

and not *you*?"
Camille shrugs.
"I'm pretty sure it's due
to the other day in P.E.,
when I outran Sheila in the fifty-yard dash,
and Tommy shouted:
'Man, Camille! You're fast!'"

"So what!?" I say.

"Well, afterward, Sheila trotted over
and added, 'Fast like a four-legged beast!'"

"What did *you* say to her?"

"I think I just agreed."

For a brief moment,
hurt makes its home on Camille's face,
a vulnerability I've never seen.
And in that second, I really get it.
Like me, Camille struggles,
but in her own way, and in that—
*we are not alone.*

I drape my arm
around her shoulder
and squeeze.

Just then
the bus driver
regards us in the mirror
and winks
like it's exactly
the lightness
we need.

## 132.

Whenever the phone rings,
Mom and I race to get it, spilling things,
bumping into furniture,
and tripping over each other.

I have a bruise
on my right hip
from an encounter
with a table.

This time,
the phone rings three times
by the time I grab the receiver
and pull it to my ear,
all breathless:

"Hello? Hello?"

A slight delay—

"Abbey the Artist!

It's Dad."
*IT'S REALLY HIM!*

Finally after all these days, I catch my breath.

We small-talk
about the snow, groundhogs, and other things,
which is strange
since there's much bigger stuff to say.

And then
it just happens—

He opens up to me.

"Abbey . . . I know it's not easy,
moving so much and all these new towns
and schools, making new friends each time,
and now I'm gone
at such an important time
in your life—"

        "It's okay, Dad," I manage.

"When I come home, I promise
I'll spend more time with you.
I want . . . to get to know you better,
to be closer. We could do stuff together."

        "I'd like that."

        "One of the guys here told me about
an art museum in Atlanta.
Maybe we could go?"

"Okay," I whisper, smiling and shaking.

Then the words just come pouring out,
            and I say it without regret, like I'm six again,
                    like these might be our last words:

        "I love you so much, Dad,

I'm afraid you won't come home,
and I just keep thinking about Jackson and Kate.
And Aunt Rose."

"I know, Sweetie. I know,
and I love you too."

He can't bring himself to say
that everything
*will be*
*okay.*

## 133.

It's Valentine's Day
and I am Abbey Wood,
and I have the best friend
in the universe

Camille,
who needs me like I need her,

and the coolest teacher on the planet
Mr. Lydon

and there's a boy in this town
by the name of
Jacob

who just found me by my locker
      and KISSED the side of my cheek
when no one was looking
and placed a red sketchbook
      on my stack of books—
before tripping on his backpack
at our feet.


I am Abbey Wood


who is from here and there and a bit of everywhere—
      and maybe I'm getting used to that.


      In Language Arts, I plan to doodle hearts
and decide NOT
                to attend
Sheila's
once-in-a-lifetime,
some-would-die-for,
coveted-and-prized,
by-invitation-only
party.


I'm pretty sure that night
I have a picture to draw
and a best friend to call.

## 134.

Word travels
like a shock wave
across the school
that I've said *No thanks*
to Sheila, who doesn't deal well
with rejection
of her heartfelt
invitation.

## 135.

In Math,
Lana studies me
then stabs her hand in the air:
"Ms. D, when can we switch seats?"
Then scowls at me still seated beside her
and adds, "We've been sitting
in these same lame seats
for weeks!"

## 136.

As I wait for the bus,
a fluttering catches my eye
in the tree I'd chosen for Aunt Rose,
which is skeletal now,

the yellow ribbon gone bone white,
all shredded and torn.

A Valentine balloon
flaps from the inner branches
like a heart that's forgotten to stop
a few minutes after death.

The tree isn't dead, I know,
just resting and restoring,
preparing for its buds
to reappear, and its leaves
to clothe the branches again
in spring.

I walk to the tree,
        drop my backpack on the ground,
and pull myself up onto the lowest branch,
as if I've climbed it before
or once in a dream,
or in another lifetime
maybe.

My legs and body are strong
and do exactly what I ask,
so I climb higher
        and higher still
until I can see *all* of the school—
the buses, The Trio, even Camille's red hair—

but the balloon is too high to reach,
so I stop climbing and breathe deeply;
my breath is stolen by the cold air,
and my chest is full
of longing.

My hair whips loose
across my face, and I pull it back
and smile up into the sky
and consider
how it goes
on and on
times
infinity

137.

Mr. Lydon
quizzes us about 3-D art
      and what "balance" refers to.


"It's so the thing won't tip over." Sheila giggles.


Without thinking or stopping myself,
I blurt out, "It's a way of combining elements
to give stability to a work of art."
      The last three words come out squeaky,
and my tongue struggles with "stability,"


      but at last
      I have said *something* somewhat intelligent
in my all-time favorite class,
      to my very favorite teacher.


He gives me a knowing smile:
"Fabulous, Abbey!"


—and I like him even more.


Camille goes all open-mouthed
and high-eyebrowed,
shock and pride bringing
a colorful palette to her face.

It's a small thing really—
but kinda-sorta monumental
for me,
Abbey.

138.

Life is a moody teenager,
with its ups and downs—

because later that same day
taped to my locker I discover
a neatly written list
torn from a journal or notebook
with distinctly penciled columns: **_Pretty_**     **_Ugly_**     **_Nobody_**

                Jiman and I,
along with a few others,
stand together in the land of **_Nobody_**,
and then there's Camille
with a small lineup of girls
awarded the honor of **_Ugly_**.

I can't tell by Jiman's face
if she got one too.

       I would blame the football boys for this,
*except* for the three names
listed so clearly

in solidarity
under
**Pretty**.


## 139.

I discover the same list
taped to Camille's locker
and shred it quickly into a billion pieces,
but only after the whole world
of Henley Middle
reads it.

On the tip of my tongue,
I hold back an arsenal of words,
like ammunition, for the three
who labeled my friend
so hurtfully.

But who am *I*
to stand up
to anybody?
I stand by
wordless most of the time—
or was it
*worth*less?

In other words,
*Nobody*.

140.

Speaking of words,
not a single one from Dad.
And a mood descends upon our house.

I spread his letters across my bed,
the most recent penned in blue ink,
his handwriting quivery.

*Was he tired when he wrote it,*
*or distracted? Was it dark or noisy?*

*Is the ink so recent*
*one of my tears*
*could smear his words*
*and turn my fingertips blue?*

The paper doesn't have lines
so his writing slants down
the page, as if you could shake
the paper, and the message
would slip away, forever.

I touch his words, especially the last ones,
then gather all the letters together
and close them into a box
beside my bed, for when
I might need them
one day.

## 141.

The little brother
of Jiman

sits up front on the bus.
I'm in the middle somewhere.
He plays with two action figures—
soldiers actually, positions them
on top of the seat
in front of him.

I watch
his story of war:
the soldiers clobber each other,
until one takes a fatal blow.
Then he lays them side by side,
and it's hard to tell who won
because they both appear
to be sleeping
or maybe
dying.

Flirty squeals erupt
from the back of the bus
and pull my attention away.

The Trio are all on board
with the football boys,

going to one another's houses.
At the next stop,
they shove and strut
down the aisle
all noise and hands
as one boy steals
an action figure
and pockets it for keeps.

**GIVE IT BACK!**
Jiman commands,
bolting to the front
in two seconds flat.

The driver turns in his seat,
makes eye contact with her,
nods,
and demands the boys
return what they stole,
           and puts them off the bus
for repeated offenses
for a whole week.

On the side of the road,
they stomp their feet, shove
one another, and kick the dirt.
The Trio prop their hands on cocked hips.
In the bus, the air feels different
and a slow clap begins

until the whole bus
is cheering—and Jiman
and her brother sit taller,
taller now than ever.


## 142.

So vivid I can touch him—


*Dad!*


He's in the desert . . .
and gunfire pops all around him,
like fireworks with no celebration.


He collapses into the sand
and a bearded soldier overtakes him,
stands above him, takes aim
with his gun—


I wake to screaming—
It is my own!


Mom is beside me in seconds.


She wraps her arms around me
and rocks me back and forth,
back and forth,

back and forth,
like I am an infant again.

Is it *me* who is shaking?

"I know,
        I know, Abbey," she whispers like a lullaby.

        We wake the next morning,
awkward and tired,
with dark circles for eyes.

        Mom walks me to the bathroom
where I try
to wash the nightmare
away.


143.

Camille and I poke
our squishy burgers
and grease-soaked fries
and plan our upcoming spring break.

She shares her goal to refine her near-perfect layup,
with award-winning humility.

No matter what anyone writes,
I think Camille is amazing.

"Basketball *every* day!" she sighs
and then spots Jacob
                halfway across the cafeteria.
        "HEY!" she screams, heads turning
at her volume and audacity.

        Jacob carries his tray over to us.
        He's back from a field trip.

        "Guess I'll be lunching
        with the young ones today!"

"You know you love it!" Camille beams.

I smile shyly.

        Then Camille—spontaneously—bounds away:

                "Coach! Coach! Wait up!"

Jacob and I stare after her
and grin at one another.

"So, what're *your* plans for the break?" I ask.

"Soccer practice." He shrugs.
"My dad—well, pretty much everyone—
counts on me to play."

He nods at his teammates
sitting and watching us
from a few tables over, some
I recognize from the bus.

"But you're into it, right?"

"Yeah, but between soccer and basketball,
I don't have time for anything else,
like painting or . . ." He pauses
and looks right at me.

My heart stops
          for a fraction          of a second.

"And I really miss art class," he continues.
"It's all practice these days.

"You're lucky, you know," he says,
"You *do* exactly what you want."

"I do?" I ask,
never having thought of myself like that.

"Yeah, you're good at art
and that's how you spend your time.
I can tell you love it, too."

*My friends seem to know me*
          *better than I know myself.*

"Can't you be," I suggest, "Mr. Athletic and a part-time Picasso too?"

"I guess." He smiles slowly.
        "Abbey, I really like talking to you."

"Me too, I mean—like talking to you, too!"

We finish our lunches
and slowly walk away
glancing back over our shoulders
as we head down our different
hallways.


## 144.

Time moves

        in slow motion

                during the cold months.

Everything is sluggish.

Thawing.

        Quiet.

Nothing blooms.

At least spring break is coming
and I'll be flying to stay with Gram & Gramps
in *sunny* Florida.

Mom assures me she'll be fine
alone.

"I'll spring clean,
I'll grade.
I'll be okay."

## 145.

In Camille's bedroom,
we scheme up ways to keep in touch
         over the week-long break.

*First,*

*you call me,*

      *and then I'll call you—*

*every*

    *other*

*day.*

"On your plane trip, look down
and I'll wave up at you."
Camille giggles.

"Maybe you can come with me
to Florida some time," I tell her.
"Or South Carolina and meet
my friend Makayla—although she
might've moved by now, too."

"That'd be cool. As you know,
I've never been anywhere
                      but Here-Town."

"Stick with me—and you'll get
a small taste of Everywheres-ville."


146.

On the plane,
I sketch and doodle,
feeling mature traveling alone,
in my window seat with my peanuts—
even though the attendant
keeps checking up on me
every twenty minutes.

Gram & Gramps
meet me at the baggage claim,
waving like fragile, tan maniacs.

I feel insignificant
but safe in the back seat
of their tank-like
grandparent car.

I set up camp in Dad's boyish
bedroom. It's the first time
I've visited by myself.
Usually, we stay at a motel
down the street.

I browse Dad's books
and his superheroes—dusty
but still positioned on shelves,
ready to take on the world.

## 147.

It's peaceful
with Gram & Gramps.

Their house has two decks,
and the breeze from the sea
comes freely through their screens.

They read the newspaper
for the first half of each day,
and eat slowly—foods like grapefruit,
poached eggs, and dry toast. Their coffee
lasts all morning. I lounge around,
reading magazines and drawing,
popping on my flip-flops
to wander the beach.

My seashell collection grows
over the course of the week,
my pockets sag with their weight.

Each afternoon, I spread out a towel
near a dune, so I'm mostly hidden,
and position my sketchbook so I can capture
              the waves,
                     the sky,
                            beach birds,
                                 a kite,
                                        people walking along the shore.

At night, I sleep downstairs,
with Gram & Gramps above me.
I can step right out of Dad's room
                                and onto the lower deck.

The ocean sings its soothing tune,
so each evening I'm lulled to sleep

in the place where Dad slept
when he was a little boy,
listening to the same
watery song.


## 148.

Gramps suggests
I type Dad a letter
       on his snail of a computer.

"But sometimes I don't know what to tell him," I stall.

Mostly, I mean:
I don't know what to say *in letters* to him,
especially letters to him when
he's at war, and every word
must count, must mean
something.

Gram overhears. "That's natural, sweetheart."
She thinks it's a father-daughter thing.

       But it's been a while
              since I stopped crawling into his lap
for his comfort.

At some point, we must've

silently agreed

I'd outgrown that kind of thing.

And now, like Mom said,
I'm on the *brink of womanhood*—
or something like that.

So along with my pathetic attempt at a letter,
we enclose one of my sketches
of Dad's boyhood home
with the sun shining
protective and golden
above it.


## 149.

Toward the end of my break,
Gram calls me to her:
"I want to show you something."

She drags a box from under Dad's bed
and pulls from it
several large pieces of paper.

Instantly, I know it's artwork.
Made by my very own dad!

Not because it's from under *his* bed,
but because I recognize
the way he *would* draw and paint
*if* he drew and painted.

*It's familiar somehow.*

"Why didn't he tell me about this?" I ask in disbelief.
        "And where exactly was his easel all these years?"

Gram just murmurs something
about the past being the past to my dad.

We study the drawings and paintings,
Gram reminiscing about each
and telling me stories about when
or why he made it.

Then eventually, while packing
it all back up, she hands me
a stack of homemade books.

"Comics too?" I demand,
like an urchin coming out of
my shell.

## 150.

The next morning,
I can't put Dad's comics down.
While chewing my toast,
I ask Gram why he stopped.

She considers me,
takes her time sweetening her second cup of coffee,
and then finally admits,
"He had big plans for his art."

"Who knew he was *even* creative!"
Still, I'm clearly in awe.

My lunch conversation
with Jacob pops into my head
about making time for art

and I demand to know: "Why did Dad give it up?"

"Because . . ." Gram stalls
and then she begins again,

"He and your mom had *you*,
and you were more important to him than anything,
so he moved on."

"Then it's because of *me* that he's in the Army . . .
and in Afghanistan right now?"

"Oh no, honey," Gramps jumps in,
joining our conversation,
"He just did the *right* thing,
that's all."

## 151.

Later,
on the beach
I question a world
where doing the right thing
means giving up
the things you
love.

## 152.

A week later
and a little more freckled,
it's back to Mom
and my quiet bedroom,
back to school,
back to Jacob
and Camille.

On the way to my locker, I notice my shoes
still have grains of sand in them

and with each step,
I can almost feel the shifting dunes beneath my feet.

I picture Dad's artwork and comics,
picture Dad out there somewhere

across the world,
sleeping or fighting
in a faraway desert,
or doing whatever he does,
    and I wonder
if *he* has sand in his boots too,
and if each step he takes
he thinks
of Mom,
and
of me.

# APRIL

........................................................................

## 153.

It's been raining for days now,
and everything is growing greener.

The flowers and trees are blooming,
and Mom and I take turns X-ing off
the days we pass without Dad—
      or each day until he comes back to us.

We haven't heard from him in weeks
      in this hopeful
            blossoming
               missing
                   maddening
                       season.

## 154.

Mom and I don't mention

    *not*

    hearing from Dad.

I sense it's getting serious.
It's been too long in between.

The days

    tick
    tick
    tick by

      too loudly.

We talk about him like he's here:

    "Dad's show is on TV!" I announce.
    "Let's have Dad's favorite dinner tonight," she says.

But we spend more time
        in our separate bedrooms,

    missing him
    and
    acting like
it's
no
big
THING.

155.

Two important things happen today.

ONE:
All the girls have been pulled
from class to visit the nurse
and talk about
*Our Bodies.*

Sheila, Angela, and Lana are painting their fingernails.
They must know all this already.

The nurse explains how girls
can get pregnant after starting their periods—and I think
she means to scare us

yet the following stunning revelation floods me:

*I* can CREATE life one day
        if I choose to.
        When I'm ready.

        *It is a gift.*

But for now,
ART is my gift,
how I create,
how I cope
with this world.

TWO:

The Trio find Camille in the hall afterward.

Tommy and a few boys loom nearby.

I know because they holler, "Whoa, slow down, Army!"

as I make a beeline for them.

"None of that stuff applies to you, Camille," they say,

"'cause no boy's ever going to want *you*!"

That's when I totally lose it—or find it.

My VOICE!

And I use it:

"Self-worth is *NOT*

people *wanting* you.

It's what's *INSIDE* of you!

And Camille is beautiful—

inside and out.

Go!

Examine!

Yourselves!"

So—yeah—perhaps it's a little over their heads.

"Who does she think *she* is?" Sheila snips.

Lana and Angela raise their eyebrows

and purse their lips.

But I know.

*I know who I am.*

And it works. The Trio disperse—
or maybe the bell rings.

Either way
I'm counting it as a win,
since they leave Camille and me alone
to bask in my
long-time-coming
vocally
valiant
victory.

## 156.

I decide to talk to Mom
about my day, my revelation,
while she's driving.
It's less awkward that way,
but I'm having trouble putting into words
how I feel about art and what happened with Camille
when we come to a halt.

A small crowd has formed
on the side of the road.

Signs shout,
thrust above heads:
>       *Choose Peace!*
>       *One Tragedy Is Enough!*

*Not My War!*
Chanting voices
Angry fists
Open mouths
now surrounding our car:
*WE*
*DON'T*
*WANT*
*THIS*
*WAR!*
Mom drives through it,
and they part
but want to know:

> *Thumbs up or down?*
> *Honk twice to agree.*
> *With them? Or against them?*

Mom doesn't speak.
She stares straight ahead
biting her lip
gripping the wheel
through the heart of the crowd
where suddenly I spot Camille's dad,
with a peace sign on his chest
and intent on his face.
We lock eyes
and my hand waves
before I can stop it
from this small act
of betrayal
to Dad.

## 157.

"There have been casualties," the news anchor announces.
—or maybe we received the news through a phone call,
or heard it from a family friend,
or maybe it was in the air
like spring pollen

or poison,
or chemicals
of mass destruction.

"Casualties."
Mom clicks off the TV and radio, and closes out
our computer's news page.

*Casualties.*

*Am I being punished for waving my hand?*
*For the doubts I've had about war?*

Mom grabs the phone, punches numbers frantically,
calling everyone she knows,
then slams the receiver down and sinks to her knees.
"Casualties," she sobs.

I stare at the walls
which stare back
at me.

## 158.

The
*not knowing*
may have lasted
a solitary
dark
hour.

## 159.

It may have lasted

      an eternity of twenty-four.

  It may have lasted

        several sleepless days.

    But it felt like

      YEARS.

160.

. . . until we finally receive word from the base

*It's not him!*

## 161.

It's no ONE we know.

*Knew.*

Which is reason to breathe again, smile, even laugh at first
out of relief,

but . . . it's *someONE.*

The names are like anyONE's,
like someONE's uncle,
like Angela's brother,
like someONE's friend.

Now that family has a memorial
instead of a father,

a flag
instead of a brother.

Perfectly folded
and triangular,
red,
white,
and
blue.

he's sorry. He knows we were worried.
    He thinks maybe
    he'll be able to stay in touch
    a little better now."

## 162.

The phone rings
extra early the next morning.

My eyes snap open.

I know
it's *him*.

Mom's crying

    and whispering,

       "I was so . . . scared! And Abbey—"

and gasping.

I stand in her doorway.
She notices me.

"Okay, okay,"
she says quickly
and replaces the receiver.

"He had only a minute.
But he told me to tell you he loves you—

163.

Puberty—
      is a wicked initiation
      to the rest of my life,
      but I'm surviving
      this club of *adolescence*.


        Not to mention
        seventh—the worst of all grades
     and a brand-new school,
and all that's happened this year.

Finally, at last,
we're assembling our end-of-the-year art portfolios.

And I add my favorite pieces,
inspecting my first self-portrait with hesitation,
before including it.

      Is *this* really still me?

Mr. Lydon flips through my work
and smiles encouragingly:

      "Keep it up this summer, Abbey.
        You're really going somewhere!"

And I startle at his words
and wonder if he knows
if my family will be relocating soon.

Then—*Duh!*
I get what he means.
"Thanks, Mr. Lydon,

                    thank you for everything!"

# 164.

This month,
my period arrives like anything—
the rain, like the nighttime,
like my next breath
of air.

I'm not even surprised
or angry about it.

Maybe—
and I mean maybe—still undecided,
but maybe
it's a gift.

What's more, I miss Aunt Rose,
but I'm getting used to the idea
of her gone now

        and I wonder

how Jackson and Kate
would feel
about this.

At the moment,
I can hold the sadness
because I know it will
be replaced by joy—
the way war and peace
and summer and winter
and good and bad
turn 'round and 'round
each other.

## 165.

Camille and I
spend our afternoons at her house
or mine,
studying for
our final tests.

At Camille's,
Jacob always drops by
and lingers.

When he does,
I cannot remember
anything
I've learned all year.

Except the color
of his eyes and the dimple
when he smiles, and his kind
hands, and how he's a good friend
to Camille, and how he thinks for himself,
and the kiss he placed on my cheek.
                    But none
of this will be on these tests—
or I'd most definitely,
most certainly
pass.

### 166.

*Dear Dad,*

*It was so good—for Mom—to hear your voice.*
*Gram showed me your artwork over spring break.*
*(I hope you don't mind.)*

*Maybe you can draw again one day.*

*By the way, I love your easel!*

*Guess what? I drew a comic for my portfolio*
*about a boy who becomes a soldier.*

*Love,*
*Abbey*

## 167.

Lying flat on my bed,
I balance Mr. Poodle on one foot up in the air
and the camo poodle Dad gave me
on the other.

I conjure up fateful things like:

*If Mr. Poodle falls off first,*
*then Dad will come home unhurt.*

and

*If the camo poodle falls off first,*
*then something else will happen—*

      but I shut my eyes to block that thought.

      When he does come home,
I have so much to ask him,
so much I want to know.

*I have missed him so.*

## 168.

*Dear Abbey,*

*Your artwork rocks!*

*I can't wait to spend more time with you and Mom.*

*I'm sorry for being gone—BEFORE and now.*

*This may sound crazy, with me so far away,*
*but I feel like we've grown closer somehow*
*while I've been gone. I should be home*
*soon after your school year ends.*

*Love,*
*Dad*

## 169.

Camille shoots layups,
and I sprawl on her driveway
surrounded by tubes of paint.

My canvas is a pair of high-tops.
Naturally, she's requested peace signs
and basketballs—no surprise!

I line up her name across the front
and paint stripes on the tongues
and my initials on her soles.

*I'm afraid I could get used to this.*

*Living here.*

*Having a forever friend like Camille.*

I'm thinking this when Camille's dad
comes outside. I picture him at the protest,
but he doesn't mention it. Instead he says,
"Abbey, your dad's been in our thoughts.
We're looking forward to his safe return."
And as simple as that, he heads off
to mow their grass.

I was holding
my breath. Now I'm breathing again
a sigh of relief when Camille says,
"It's not the end of the world, Abbey,
when adults disagree."

     Camille and I make plans for summer—
painting, swimming, and basketball.
    We're getting started *right now*
    just in case
    my family
    has to move.

## 170.

Mom has dropped me off
at the downtown
               *Art Supply Store*

I need a canvas and new paints
for Dad's Homecoming,
which should occur

any
     day
          now.

I'm in my element, and I'm happy
     as I reach for a tube of paint
for the painting I have in mind,
and out of the corner of my eye,
I notice someone directly beside me.
We reach for the exact same tube
at the exact same time.

               *It is Jiman!*

She's probably not sure
what to make of me since
no words live in my head.
     *Words, what are words?*
*I cannot remember even one.*

"What are you painting?" she leads.

*Breathe, Abbey! Just breathe.*

"A painting for my dad," I manage,

and

"You?"

"A mural for my parents' restaurant,"
she says in a quiet matter of fact.

Side by side, we stare at paints.

I could tell her
that my family ate at their restaurant,
that I'd like to see her mural when it's done,
that I think she's awesome.

"You know . . .
they called *me* names too,"
she says.

I take another deep breath,
know she's talking about
the boys on the bus—
or maybe The Trio,
or both.

"They get bored eventually,"
she says.
"Besides . . .
we belong here, you and I."

At first I think she means
the art store—but quickly realize
she means so much more.

And I let her words sink in
like seeds planted in fertile dirt.

Then, for some reason, I tell her,
"You're a really good sister, Jiman."

A crooked smile leaps to her face.

"My name is Abbey," I continue,
feeling courageous now.

"I know." She laughs.

            "Where are you from?" I ask her.

"My family is Kurdish,
but I was born and raised in New Jersey.
What about you?"

My answer is complicated, too.
"I'm kind of from a lot of places.
I can tell you about it sometime."

We stare at each other briefly, as if
we both know we're going to be friends.

Sometimes it takes an eternity to figure things out,
especially when you're in middle school.

We start to turn away at the exact same time,
        but I turn back and take a risk:

"Do you want to come over one day?
We could paint."

## 171.

The next day on the bus
Jiman tells me a story,
set in our art class:

> *It started with a single dot*
> *that I turned into a sun.*

Appear the antagonists:

> *They walk past when Mr. Lydon isn't looking,*
> *hands at their sides, marker or pen uncapped,*
> *and stab it or drag it*
> *across my paper.*

I'm on the edge of my seat:

> *Once or twice, when I crumpled it up,*
> *they laughed when I started over, called me a name.*
> *But I realized I was letting them win.*

And the hero triumphs:

> *Now, I can transform any mark or mean word*
> *into a butterfly, flower, or bird.*
> *It's how I learned I'm talented.*

With a twist:

> *I had a feeling, Abbey,*
> *that you'd be fine too.*

The end!
     or
The beginning . . .

## 172.

The last day of school
begins in an ordinary square classroom
with blue walls, a white board, a striped flag
forever tied in my mind to September 11th, 2001—
the one school I'll always
remember.

## 173.

Other students fill the desks
around me, and as attendance is taken,
and the final announcements are made,
I know I'm different.

Words roll from my tongue, the ones
I've repeated since I was five:

>      . . . *with liberty and justice for all.*

But today,

>           my eyes are open wide.

>           I will stand up to things that are wrong
let myself be heard, be strong, defend,
befriend. I can do things I never realized.
I have skills that travel.

I pledge allegiance.
>      I pledge allegiance.
>           I pledge allegiance
>      to stand up,
>      to stand tall,
>      to mean it

wherever I am
>      *with liberty and justice for all.*

174.

To make my room
less temporary, Camille, Jacob, and Jiman have agreed
to help transform my ceiling into art.
Jacob skips soccer for this!

It takes two minutes tops
before Jiman wins the hearts
of my other two friends.

　　　Mom's on board with our project,
and she's stocked us with all the supplies.

I've decided to go with deep blue
and stars that pierce through,
shining into this world from another,
which makes me think of Aunt Rose.

Jiman designs elaborate stars
like Georgia O'Keeffe flowers.

And Jacob freestyles constellations.
"Go Michelangelo!" I tease.

"Doing all the hard work for you guys,"
Camille reminds us, as she layers blue
into the four corners of the room.

When we're done,
we all recline on my bed
to stargaze at our creation.
And I consider myself lucky
to be among friends,
which is a really good place
to be.

# AND THE MONTHS BEYOND

175.

Dad has begun the process
of coming home to us.

It will take weeks.

But a few more weeks we can manage now.

Just enough time to finish
        my painting for him.

On the phone, I ask him quietly,

"Has it been bad?"

        but not: *Will you be the same?*

And he whispers,
"Abbey, I'm fortunate,
I get to come home to my two favorite girls."

And his voice sounds like liquid
somewhere out there

on the other side of the world.

## 176.

Then,

it just happens.

*Finally!*

The door opens and closes,
and he is back where he should be,
back where he belongs,
back to the place where we all sleep,
sharing the same latitude
and longitude on a map.

It's as simple as that.
There are no other words.

Just—
*the three of us*
*together*
*in the same place*
*at the same time*
*again.*

For now,

                we are home.

We are.

## 177.

Within days,
it's *almost* like he was never gone.

    *Almost.*

      Some things *are* different now.
I'm not exactly sure how.
I can't put it onto the page
or paint it into a picture—
not yet.

I can see it in his eyes.
There is helplessness and protectiveness.
There is strength and weakness.
There is loss and there is love.

Maybe the difference is Dad,
maybe it's me,
maybe it's Aunt Rose,
maybe it's Mom,
maybe it's War.

We have shifted
as our world has,
forever scarred.
But we are together
and we are stronger.

178.

Instead of sitting around,
Dad seems anxious to connect,
to be a family again.

"I have some stuff to show you," Dad tells me one afternoon

and pulls the artwork
I sent to him in Afghanistan
from his boxes.

Each one is carefully packaged
and unbent. He takes his time
displaying them
on his bed.

But I can't wait any longer
and have to ask:
"Why didn't you tell me you were an artist, too?"

"That was a long time ago, Abbey,
and *you* are my masterpiece,"
he says, looking into my eyes.

My knees go weak
with the weight of his love.

Then he takes out
a folder full of drawings
that *aren't* mine.

In response to each picture I sent,
there's another one,
like an echo, or an answer,
or maybe a question.

There are several desert scenes
and pictures of soldiers
and children.

"Her name is Amena."
He points to a sketch of an Afghan girl.

"I think I just took a break from art," he explains.

I study his pictures,
admiring his talent.

"But your art *and* mine helped me to get by, to survive."

Then Mom comes over to us.
Dad pulls her close to one side
and me to
his other.

## 179.

Mom seems more like her old self.
I take a chance as we're driving past Henley
and ask if she wants to meet Aunt Rose's tree.
At first, she shakes her head vehemently,
but after a mile she turns around,
drives back, sighs, and whispers, "Show me."
The ribbon is completely gone and the tree wears
leaves now. Mom surprises me and reaches her hands
up to a low branch and swings from it like a child.
We giggle when she slips and falls, and sit together
beneath it for a while. She doesn't say she's sorry
for the year I've had—it's been hard on everyone—
but I can see pride and love and an apology
shining in her hope-filled eyes.

180.

*Self-Portrait Revisited*

I leave an expanse

of

      white

space

I am a work in progress

*Abbey*

# AUTHOR'S NOTE

As a teacher, I'm often surprised by how my middle-schoolers have heard of 9/11 but cannot comprehend its magnitude. This is no wonder, since some of their lives' tragedies have yet to be written. But it's a story that needs to be told and retold through many voices. It's a tragedy both shared and uniquely personal.

Like Abbey, the main character of *The Places We Sleep*, I was not in New York City on September 11, 2001. Like Abbey, I live in the South. Yet the reverberations of that day were far and wide.

On that indescribable morning, nineteen militants associated with al-Qaeda, an Islamic extremist group, hijacked airplanes and used them as weapons against targets in the United States. Nearly three thousand people in New York City; Washington, D.C.; and Pennsylvania lost their lives that day.

At the time, I was pregnant with my first child. In the days and weeks that followed the terrorist attacks, I felt a deep fear of bringing a child into a world where such death and destruction could occur. Furthermore, my two brothers and my brother-in-law were deployed to Afghanistan and Iraq in the subsequent war.

As I cared for my infant and continued, along with the nation, to process the events of 2001, I began writing Abbey's story, which unfolded in verse. I was not necessarily writing a novel, but finding a way of creatively coping and working through a new unfamiliar sense of foreboding.

Since 2001, my daughter has blossomed into a complicated teenager, for whom puberty may sometimes seem like the greatest tragedy. Having a child renewed my faith in the goodness of the world. In fact, I now recognize that bringing a human being into the world is a courageous act of hope.

For Abbey, adolescence coincides with the uncertainties of an entire nation. What was it like to come of age at a time when no one felt secure? When prejudices bubbled and strengthened just beneath the surface of one's skin? When the diversity at the heart of a nation became a source of tension? Is it so different today?

Maybe Abbey's story can inspire others to choose kindness and tolerance, to learn one another's names, to opt for creation over destruction. If nothing more, I hope Abbey inspires others to express themselves through poetry and art.

— Caroline

# ACKNOWLEDGMENTS

I'm grateful for this opportunity to thank those who've helped me to become a writer and now an author. This book would not exist without you!

Thank you to Richard, the love of my life, for your lyrical collaborations and shared joie de vivre, and to Rose, with whom I was pregnant on 9/11 and who inspired me to tell this story, and to Rowan, my own personal big shot and spirited fan. Many aspiring writers and artists don't have the support of their family, but you have always believed in me and my dream of becoming an author, even when it seemed impossible or inconvenient. Thank you, sweet family!

To my extended family, thank you for providing me with years of unconditional love and support and, whether you were aware of it or not, fodder for stories.

To my friends who've motivated and encouraged me to keep writing, a little part of you is in all I write: Rhonda Stansberry, Kathy Dykes, Jill Thomson, Hosanna Banks, Amy Ridings, and Diane Lewis.

Thank you to my brothers, James and Jason Brooks; my brother-in-law, Chris DuBois; my father-in-law, Charles DuBois; and my grandfathers, Carroll Quinn and James Brooks Sr. for your military service. You were the inspiration for Abbey's dad.

Thank you to my editor, Sally Morgridge. Your experience as an NYC middle-schooler during 9/11 lent a beautiful vision to Abbey and brought out the best versions of my characters. Thank you to the lovely staff at Holiday House, especially art director Kerry Martin, for making this story into a real-live book. Thank you to my agent, Louise Fury, for your dedication and tenaciousness. Your steadfast belief in my manuscript has buoyed me more than once! Kathrin Honesta, the cover art is breathtaking—thank you! And a special thank you to my sensitivity reader for insight and perspective into key ways to improve this book.

Thank you to those who've read my manuscript, in part or in its entirety: Lynne Berry, Rebecca Brooks, Lisa Connor, Richard DuBois, Rose DuBois, Susan Eaddy, Margaret Fusco, Heather Hale, Diane Lewis, and Amy Parker. Some of these poems have existed in various versions, so please forgive me if I've forgotten anyone else who's read them over the years.

The multiple critique groups I've been fortunate enough to be a part of have been integral to my growth as a writer. To the P-Gals from UMass MFA, I'm still moved by your poetry and magic: Kristin Bock, Pam Burdak, Carrie Comer, Robyn Heisey, Caroline Lewis, Judy Nacca, Karen Skolfield, and Sam Wood. Lynne Berry and Susan Eaddy, my first kidlit group, you taught me so much! Thank you Midsouth SCBWI, you rock! A shout-out goes to my former East Nashville group before several of you flew away to faraway locales: Kimberly Dana, Meg Griswold, Molly McCaffrey, and Linda McMunn. To fellow writer Heather Hale, thank you for your timely and tireless reads of this book, daring and thoughtful feedback, and kinship and friendship in general. I'm so glad we met!

Thank you to all the teachers who've challenged me to become a better writer and decent person. Nancy Stewart, Catherine Sniderman, Bonnie Auslander, Rosa Shand, John Bird, and Dara Wier, you have all showed me the beauty of words. Thank you to my family members who were teachers by profession. You inspired me to become both a teacher and writer: Nancy Dellinger, Camilla Quinn, Mark Quinn, and Glenda Wallace. And finally, thank you to my first teachers, my parents, Jim and Rebecca Brooks, who taught me to be curious about the world and to believe in myself.

Though *The Places We Sleep* is more of a coming-of-age story than a 9/11 story, I hope it honors all who were impacted by the myriad of tragedies on that day and in the months and years beyond. I would like to acknowledge and praise the police officers, firefighters, first responders, EMTs, doctors, and countless involved civilians, as well as all military personnel and their families. There are so many small acts of heroism in the face of tragedy, so an additional thank you to all of the unsung heroes surrounding 9/11.